God Bless the Trappers

Tranay Adams

Lock Down Publications and Ca$h Presents

God Bless the Trappers

A Novel by *Tranay Adams*

Tranay Adams

Lock Down Publications
P.O. Box 870494
Mesquite, Tx 75187

Visit our website @
www.lockdownpublications.com

Lock Down Publications
Like our page on Facebook: Lock Down Publications @
www.facebook.com/lockdownpublications.ldp
Cover design and layout by: **Dynasty Cover Me**
Book interior design by: **Shawn Walker**

Stay Connected with Us!

Text **LOCKDOWN** to 22828 to stay up-to-date with new
releases, sneak peaks, contests and more…
Thank you.

Submission Guideline.

Submit the first three chapters of your completed manuscript to ldpsubmissions@gmail.com, subject line: Your book's title. The manuscript must be in a .doc file and sent as an attachment. Document should be in Times New Roman, double spaced and in size 12 font. Also, provide your synopsis and full contact information. If sending multiple submissions, they must each be in a separate email.

Have a story but no way to send it electronically? You can still submit to LDP/Ca$h Presents. Send in the first three chapters, written or typed, of your completed manuscript to:

LDP: Submissions Dept
Po Box 870494
Mesquite, Tx 75187

DO NOT send original manuscript. Must be a duplicate.

Provide your synopsis and a cover letter containing your full contact information.

Thanks for considering LDP and Ca$h Presents.

ACKNOWLEDGEMENTS

Dorothea Creamer, Tamara Greene, Roneisha Cooper, Lashawn Green, Monique Williams, Christine Ms. Gemini, Sharon Bell, Jane Pannella, Viola King, Eliza Tellis, Natasha Friday, Standifur aka Fee, Michelle Harvey, Joan Brooks, Milly Ann, Jeannette Frazier, Delores Miles, Denise Moore, Erica Jackson, Quanisha Goss, Tracy Spicer, Genova Rhodes, Tanya Gary, Judy Richburg, Adaryl Fisher, Alesha Kream, Nikki Hamilton, Larry L-Boogie Deadmon, Melissa Nicholson, Cyndy Twin, JS Queen, Diane Wilson, LaTasha Williams, Pamela Johnston Ward, Stephanie McL The Beast Reader, Michelle Chatman, Audreina Robinson, Desto ElGato. If I missed anyone, don't wet that shit. I'll get you on the next one, pimp's fuck up, too.

Big Shout out to my sista from The Boot, I fux witchu hard body, Kim LeBlanc, my nigga fa' sho'. Tadowl!

Dedicated to Jasmine 'Choc' Devonish

I want to go to the top of the mountains and just scream.
I'm in love, so in love, met the girl of my dreams.
I won't lie. I won't front. You're who I want, who I need.
Without you, there's no me, you're The Air I Breathe.

I love you, baby. Thank you for loving me when I could not
love myself.

-Papi

Hopin' my true mothafuckas know, this be the realest shit I ever wrote.

-2pac

Tranay Adams

CHAPTER ONE

Odette made her way across the parking lot of Northgate Supermarket, en route to her Honda while holding a brown paper bag of groceries in her hands. Following behind her was a light skinned nigga of average height. He was wearing a doo-rag and a white t-shirt with Levi's hanging halfway off his ass. Odette sucked her teeth and rolled her eyes in annoyance. Homeboy had been trying to holler at her since she was standing in line waiting to pay for her food. She tried to tell him that she wasn't interested nicely, but the mothafucka wouldn't take no for an answer. He just kept coming at her, thinking that she was playing hard to get. Like most niggaz that tried to get at her, she knew that he was after one thing. Pussy. She also knew off top what had attracted his old dusty ass too. It was the fact that she was a petite woman with an ass that sat up on her back and breasts the size of two ripe melons. She didn't know what it was about short women but, for some reason, men loved ramming dick up in them. If she had to guess for herself, she'd say that they loved dominating them in bed and being able to adjust them to their liking. You know, man handling their little asses.

"Sup witchu, lil' momma? Why you ain't tryna give a nigga no play?" the nigga in the doo-rag asked, boasting his chipped front tooth. He eyed her bodacious ass hungrily and licked his big lips, thinking of all the freaky shit he could do to her little ass.

"Damn, Cuz, I'd hit this lil' bitch raw and bust up all in her shit, too. She got that lil' stanky leg walk, too. I know that pussy fiyah as a mothafucka!" he said as he rubbed his hands together mischievously.

"It ain't that. I got a man."

"That's cool. Oh, what chu can't have friends? Yo' nigga that insecure?" He had an expression on his face like, dammmnnnn, as if he couldn't imagine her fucking with a nigga like that.

"Nah, he doesn't do that male friend shit and I don't blame him. Most niggaz just be trying to smash anyway."

Like yo' old thirsty ass is trying to do now, nigga.

"Besides, I don't play that shit either. My nigga can't have no bitches as his friends," she said as she popped the trunk of her car and dropped the brown bag inside of it. "I'm the only bitch he needs on his team. You feel me?" She slammed the trunk shut and caught him staring at her ass, still rubbing his hands together. The look that he was giving her made her want to throw up. She could literally feel herself cringe, feeling him molest her with his eyes. Growing up, she always hated having a big old booty. Niggaz was pussy hounds and would always make sly comments about what they would do to her sexually. On top of that, she never knew when a nigga was trying to talk to her because he wanted more than just sex with her. She faced this obstacle all her life, which made her suspicious of men. She gave every nigga that tried to holler at her the side eye and wondered what their true intentions were.

Mothafuckaz had made her insecure about her body, which was why she tried to cover herself up as much as possible. It always felt like all eyes were on her. Now, for some women, they'd loved all that attention, but not her. Nah, she truly loathed it.

Odette thought about getting surgery to reduce the size of her breasts and her buttocks, but she didn't want to go under the knife, for fear of never coming back out alive. If it wasn't for this, then she would have gone through the surgery years ago. Until she could get over her fear, she'd just have to deal with all the bullshit that comes with being a voluptuous woman.

"I'm sayin' though, what cho man don't know won't hurt him." He bit down on his bottom lip and shook his head, thinking of how he'd hit her from the back doggy-style. He saw himself pounding her out and watching the rippling effect in her butt while he was doing so.

That does it. I'm tired of this mothafucka, yo.

Odette rolled her eyes again and exhaled, nostrils flaring. "Look, I tried to be nice, but I see the shit ain't working. So, I'm going to tell you how it is, straight up, boo boo! I don't like you! You're not my type. I am not trying to fuck with you like that. For real, for real! Damn, nigga, get a fucking clue, why don't you!" She adjusted the strap of her purse on her shoulder and tried to walk off, but he aggressively grabbed her by her arm. Eyebrows sloped and nose crinkled, he yanked her around violently so that she'd be facing him. He was so close up on her that she could smell the weed and Hennessy seeping out of his pores. She didn't notice before, but his eyes were glassy and red webbed and his lips were peeled back in a sneer.

"Ol' stuck up, high sidity, bitch! Fuck you think you talkin' to, huh? Huh?" he asked as he jerked her arm hard. He was squeezing her arm so tight that it felt like he was cutting off her blood circulation. His grip was hurting so much that she grimaced.

"Let me the fuck go." Odette tried yanking her arm away from him, but she couldn't get free of his vicelike grip.

"Shut cho ass u… aaaaah!"

Odette gritted her teeth and whipped out a can of mace from out of her purse, spraying his ass flush in the eyes. He squeezed his eyelids shut and screamed loud as hell, bringing his calloused hands to his face.

"You fuckin' bitch! You sprayed me, you fuckin' slore!" he spat with animosity, spit flying from off his lips. He swung at her blindly, but she backed out of the way of his attack.

"I got your bitch right here, nigga!" She cocked back her leg and kicked him as hard as she could in the crotch. Bystanders cringed and turned their heads, grabbing their crotches while feeling homeboy's pain.

The nigga in the doo-rag eyes bulged and his mouth dropped open. He grabbed himself and fell off to the side, balling up like a fetus inside of a womb. He squeezed his eyelids shut and gritted his teeth, trying to fight back the pain he was feeling in his loins. Tears burst from between his eyelids and spilled down the side of his face, dripping down to the asphalt.

"That's just what yo' ass get!" Odette growled and dropped the can of mace back into her purse. She walked over to the driver side door of her Honda. She'd just opened the vehicle's door when she stopped and turned around. Looking at her victim, she got pissed off all over again and charged at him, just as he'd gotten to his knees. She cocked her leg back like she was about to attempt a field goal kick and launched her sneaker into his ribs.

"Oooooooooh!" the bystanders said in unison and exchanged glances with one another. The impact of the kick cracked homeboy's ribs and lifted him off his knees. He came back to the ground, landing hard on his face. Afterwards, Odette spat on his ass and climbed behind the wheel of her Honda, pulling out of her parking space and driving off. Adjusting the rearview mirror, she stared up at it and saw the bystanders attempting to help the nigga in the doo-rag up. He got upon his feet and ungratefully shoved some of them out of the way before limping off, holding himself.

Pulling out into Los Angeles traffic, Odette heard her cellular ringing. Looking at the caller identification, she saw her mother's name and face. She sighed and tossed her phone into the front passenger seat. She wasn't trying to talk to her mother because she never had anything nice to say. When she did talk to her, they would have a good conversation, but then she got on her negative tip saying all kinds of shit that she wasn't trying to hear. She got on her about her weight, moving so far away from home, not doing what she felt like she should do with her life. Odette only had to deal with her mother's bullshit when she didn't have a man or some nigga to kick it with. She noticed that as long as her mother had somebody, she didn't have time to be all up in her business. She knew that when her mother did have a dude, she'd be as quiet as a church mouse. She and her sister, Shonda, wouldn't hear so much as a peep from her.

Odette's cellphone stopped ringing and started back up again, but she ignored it. It was her worrisome ass mother again. When the ringing stopped, it started right back up. This pissed Odette off and she snatched her cellular from off the passenger seat.

"What the fuck, mommy? I'm not trying to talk to yo' ass, especially with what you said to me. Hell, it's your ass that finally got me to get up out of C.T., anyway." She pressed *ignore* and turned her cell on *silent,* so she wouldn't have to hear the device's annoying ringing.

"These Cali niggaz are worse than the ones back home. Fucking barbarians think they can just take any bitch that they want; club a bitch over the head and drag her on home," Odette spoke aloud like someone was riding shotgun in her car while shaking her head, thinking of old boy that she'd maced and stomped out.

Odette held firmly to the steering wheel with one hand, while using the other to plug up the auxiliary cord of her iPod into her Boss stereo system. Looking back and forth between the windshield and the screen of her small silver, rectangle shaped device. She searched through the songs until she found the one that she was looking for, Musiq

Soulchild's *Love.* She pressed play and waited for the harmonious song to flood the interior of her vehicle.

Love
So many things I've got to tell you
But I'm afraid I don't know how
Cause there's a possibility
You'll look at me differently
Love
Ever since the first moment I spoke your name
From then on, I knew that by you being in my life
Things were destined to change cause

As soon the song played, Odette sat the iPod down on the front passenger seat. Afterwards, she allowed herself to get familiar with the music; it fit her mood perfectly. She nodded her head to the infectious tune and allowed the artist's lyrics to sink into her mental. Pulling up to a red stoplight, she continued to nod her head and take in her surroundings.

She saw an old couple sitting at the bus stop, holding hands and kissing. Seeing that his lady was cold as she was, rubbing her arms, the old man removed his jacket and draped it over her shoulders. Odette looked up into her rearview mirror and saw a teenage couple riding a bicycle. The young girl was riding the handle bars while her boyfriend was peddling. They laughed and chuckled, flying down the sidewalk. The wind blew against them, ruffling their clothing. The boyfriend's baseball cap was blown crooked by the wind, so he set it right, still flying down the sidewalk.

When the couple reached the gate of a tenement, the girl hopped off the handlebars and her boyfriend brought his leg over his bike. He walked her up to the door. They stared each other in the eyes while smiling, looking nervous and shit. Suddenly, the girl pecked her boyfriend on the lips and waved bye to him, entering through the gate of her apartment complex. The boyfriend rode off on his bicycle, smiling and looking like the happiest young man in the entire world.

Odette looked to her left through the window of McDonald's. People stood around, as a young man gave his lady a beautiful red rose and removed a small burgundy box from his pocket, getting down on his knee. His lady started crying and placed her hand over the lower half of her face, like she was surprised and caught off guard by what he was doing, which was true. The young man popped the question and she must have said yes. Odette believed that was true because the young man opened the ring box and his lady outstretched her hand toward him, letting him slide the engagement ring onto her finger. Next, he rose to his feet, and they kissed romantically and hugged. The restaurant erupted in applause and cheers for the young couple.

The light turned green and Odette drove through the intersection, sighing. Her shoulders slumped and her eyes sparkled like crystal, tears accumulating in them. The tenements, stores, and apartment buildings reflected on the windshield of her ride as she navigated her way through the streets. Before she knew it, tears were sliding down her cheeks and she was sniffling. It seemed to her that she'd never find the man of her dreams, that one person that would love her unconditionally. She dealt with a few guys that she thought was the one for her, but they turned out to be something else. And she winded up being disappointed, hurt, and let down.

Odette pulled to another red stoplight and wiped her tearing eyes with the back of her fist. Looking back up, she allowed her mind to take her back to a time, a time when she had went seeking out the Lord for a favor.

Odette pulled up to the church and killed the engine of her Honda. She hopped out, slamming the door shut behind her and sliding on sunglasses. Now, it was hot that day, but that's not why she'd opted to wear sunglasses. Nah, she'd chosen to wear them because they'd hide the black eye that her husband had given her. The extra makeup she applied masked the bruising on her face.

The beating she'd gotten was courtesy of that son of a bitch, Carlos. That nigga had gotten it into his head that she was creeping with their Mexican gardener, Felipe, because she'd allowed him inside of the house for a cold glass of lemonade and a sandwich. Her reason for doing this was because it was a scorching 93 degrees outside, and the poor bastard was sweating like he was a slave picking cotton. Odette didn't want the man to pass out from the heat, so she decided to let him have a break, offering him something to eat and drink. She tried to explain this to her husband, but he wasn't trying to hear that shit. He swore on the life of him that they were up in there fucking.

When Carlos saw a sweaty Felipe coming out of the house with his wife beater clinging to him, he parked his car on the front lawn and hopped out. He whipped Felipe's ass and grabbed a rake from out of the flat bed of his pickup truck, breaking it over his back. He then kicked him in his ass, sending him crashing to the ground. The pained gardener slowly got to his feet, wincing. He then limped to his truck, holding his side. Once Felipe had driven off, Carlos grabbed Odette by her hair, dragging her inside of the house kicking and screaming. Now, normally, Odette would ball up on the floor until he'd finish beating her ass, but not this time. Nah, she had some fight in her that day and enough was a mothafucking enough.

Little momma wasn't about to take an ass whipping lying down. Fuck that! She threw hands with Carlos' big ass, taking licks from him and giving him some back as *well. This was her first time fighting him back and, once it was all over, the house was a mess of broken glass and toppled furniture. After the brawl, Carlos left the house for boot camp with a busted nose and a bleeding lip. The Uber he'd requested whisked him away to his destination, while Odette got dressed and took herself to church.*

Odette hadn't stepped foot in God's domain since she was a young girl. Grandma and Grandpa Gladstone used to take her and her sister to the house of praise every Sunday. Grandma would part and comb the girls' hair, putting it in barrettes. She'd then get them dressed and spray a little of her perfume on them. Once everyone was ready to go, the girls would climb into the backseat of Grandpa's black on black '76 Cadillac DeVille. The backseat of the old Caddy looked as big as Yankee stadium to Odette and Shonda. It was spacious and clean. You couldn't find a piece of lent inside of the vintage automobile. Grandpa loved that car, so he took damn good care of it.

The leather backseats of the classic vehicle would be hot during that time of the day. This was from the car sitting parked in the driveway beneath the blazing sun for so long, its warm rays heating up the interior of the automobile. When Odette and her sister slid into the backseat of the Cadillac, it would burn their thighs and legs. So, Grandma would have to lay Grandpa Gladstone's overcoat down across the cushioning of the leather seats, so they wouldn't get burned.

As a little girl, Odette didn't care too much for church. It seemed like they would be there forever and, just when it seemed like it was time to go, the pastor would keep on going with his long ass sermon. That's when she realized that the Holy Roller was just getting started. It wasn't always bad though. After church, while the adults would busy themselves shooting the breeze inside of the parking lot, Odette and her sister would play with the other kids. Afterwards, Grandpa and Grandma Gladstone would take the girls to Denny's. Odette adored Denny's. She'd order a tall glass of milk and a big old stack of pancakes. She loved pancakes, especially with maple syrup on them. Grandpa Gladstone would sit back with his cup of coffee, watching her devour her flap jacks. He'd chuckle because it amused him that such a small child could eat so many pancakes.

Anyway, until Odette was about thirteen years old, this was her family's Sunday ritual. It never changed, not even once. That was until Grandpa Gladstone passed away from natural causes. Grandma had found him on a Thursday night after dinner. He was inside of the garage, behind the wheel of his Cadillac DeVille, 'Diamond in the back' playing from the speakers, the exact same song he played every day on their way to church. His eyes stared blankly through the lenses of his prescription glasses and his mouth was partially open. Although he was deceased, the cigar wedged between his chubby fingers was still wafting with smoke. Winston Halbert Gladstone was buried one week later, on the same day of the week that he'd died on at Cedar Hills cemetery.

Odette came strolling through the tall double doors of the church, which had high ceilings. The Lord's house was dimly lit with the sunlight shining through the opened doors and the colorful, stained-glass windows. The colorful windows had religious figures painted on them. The pews were oak wood with padded, burgundy cushioning on the seats and backrest. The carpet was flat and gray. A burgundy rug ran from the entrance of the church to the stage where the podium resided.

Odette had gotten about halfway down the aisle when she saw the live-in maintenance man had just finished vacuuming. He looked up at her, just as he'd begun wrapping the cord around the placements at the back of the *vacuum. A smile stretched across his mole riddled, wrinkled face and expanded his thick, salt and pepper mustache across his top lip.*

"Heyyyy, Odette, I ain't seen you in a while," the maintenance man said, walking up to hug her. This was Mr. Medgar. He'd been working at the church for as long as Odette could remember. "How have you been, baby girl?" he asked, embracing her.

"I'm fine. How are you?" she asked, mustering a halfhearted smile. Considering she'd just gotten her ass beat, she wasn't really in the mood to talk to anyone. But out of love and respect for Mr. Medgar, she'd extend him that courtesy.

"Oh, I'm hanging in there. This bum leg of mine ain't slowed me down yet," he said as he smacked his weakest leg and smiled again, showcasing the gold crown on his front tooth as well as the rest of his grayish teeth. The old man had walked with a limp ever since he'd been struck by a speeding car on his way home from the supermarket one night. Ever since then, he'd been walking like he was wearing one boot.

Odette and Mr. Medgar chopped it up a little while longer before he asked was she there to see the pastor. He told her that if she was, he was in the back in his office counseling a couple that were members of the church, so she'd have to give him about an hour or so.

"Nah, I thought I'd come and get a few ticks with the Big Guy." Odette and Mr. Medgar looked up at the statue of Jesus Christ hanging on a cross on the stage. It was enormous and sitting high up, making Odette and Mr. Medgar look like children standing below it.

"Oh well, let me give you some privacy. I've gotta take out the trash and sweep out back. We're 'pose to have a BBQ this Sunday. It was nice seeing you again, Odette," he said, embracing her once again.

21

"Nice seeing you again too, Mr. Medgar." She broke
their hug and he went on about his business, pulling the
vacuum cleaner along as he pushed the cart of cleaning
items that was on the side of him.

Odette stared at Mr. Medgar's back, as he walked away
singing some old song that she was sure she'd heard
Grandpa Gladstone play in his Cadillac a couple of times
growing up. Once he'd disappeared and his crooning had
grown softer until she didn't hear it anymore, Odette took
her purse from off her shoulder and walked up the small
staircase upon the stage. Stopping before the enormous
crucifix, she got down on her knees before it and put her
hands together in prayer. Bowing her head, tears outlined
her eyelashes and slid down her cheeks. She sniffled before
she began her conversation with God's son.

"Oh, Merciful Lord, I come before you today a woman
that's broken spiritually, emotionally, as well as physically.
I don't know how I allowed this monster known as Carlos
into my life, but I have. This man has lied, cheated, abused
me, and treated me like I was crap at the bottom of his
shoe. And, yet, my dumb butt stayed with him. Not only
that. I was stupid enough to give birth to his child. Now, I
love my darling baby boy and I don't regret having him.
But, I do regret the man that I chose to have him by. I wish
I'd chosen a man that loved me unquestionably and treated
me like a jewel."

She felt herself about to break down before she could
finish. So, she took the time to gather herself before
continuing. "Father, I came to you today to ask you to
please bring me a man into my life that will honor, love,
respect, and protect me. I'm not asking for this person to be
perfect because I'm not, Father. I'm not asking for this
person to be handsome nor rich," her voice began to
crackle, so she cleared her throat, "all I ask..." She
sniffled and swallowed the lump of hurt that was in her

throat. "All I ask, Father, is for someone to love me, someone that will look at me each and every day like I am the best thing that ever happened to them, someone that will accept me with my flaws and all. That is all that I ask. I'm not asking for me to meet this man today, not even in the next week or month. I just ask that when you send him to me, Father, that he'll be for me and only me. In Jesus name I pray, Amen," And with that, Odette fell apart, sobbing and crying while holding on to the bottom half of the crucifix. After a while, she quieted down and held her position there at the lower half of the statue. Next, she cleared her throat and wiped her eyes and nose with Kleenex from out of her purse. Getting up on her knees, she slipped her sunglasses back on and headed out of the church.

A week later, Odette linked back up with Donald, her high school sweetheart, rekindling the flame that they once shared as teenagers. They dated for a time, but she realized that he wasn't the one for her. She knew that he was sleeping around with groupies on tour and he played her little mind, besides the times he hit her up when he was in town for sex. She'd gotten tired of that and broke things off with him, refusing to be just one of his booty calls for the rest of her life. They still talked though, keeping in touch over social media and the occasional phone call. As of now, they were just platonic friends.

Odette stared ahead, thinking about the day that she'd visited the church. She appeared to be in a trance from the expression on her face. It wasn't until the sound of a honking horn flooded her eardrums that she snapped out of it. Adjusting her crooked rearview mirror, she stole a glance through it and saw that there was a line of cars behind him.

"Well, damn, my bad," she said to them, but there was no way that they could hear her. Beep! Beep! Beeeeeeep!

"Fuck y'all, shit!" she said as she threw her middle finger up and out of the driver side window, mashing the gas pedal and taking off through the intersection.

Odette drove along, keeping her eyes on the road and rummaging through her purse. The stuff inside of her purse that she came across that she didn't need, she sat aside and continued her probing. Finding the electric cigarette that she was looking for, she took a pull and blew out a gust of smoke.

"I need a drink," Odette said to no one particular, scratching her forehead with her thumb. "Lemme see if sis can watch Mar Mar for a little while longer." She picked up her cellular and hit her sister up. She asked her could she watch her baby boy so she could take a moment to clear her head, and she obliged her. Smiling, Odette said, "Thanks, sis. Love you, okey dokey then, bye." Having disconnected the call, Odette tossed her cellphone onto the passenger seat and continued driving, occasionally taking a drag from her cigarette. She couldn't wait until she was sitting at the bar and telling Nigel what she wanted to drink. The alcohol was well needed to calm her nerves.

CHAPTER TWO

Kreon sat in the waiting room to see his therapist. He laid back in his seat, watching the other people that were there to see their doctors as well. There was a handful there; he couldn't help wondering what kind of lives they led. Some of them were talking among one another on their cellphones, flipping through tattered magazines, or watching the small box television set that was mounted at the high corner of the wall. Static occasionally ran across the tv's screen, but it didn't seem to bother those that were observing it. Kreon stretched and yawned, taking in all the faces of those occupying the room. He wondered if he was the craziest one present. He also pondered if they were thinking the same thing that he was.

Kreon retreated to the restroom to relieve his bladder. Standing at the urinal, he examined the graffiti that was on the wall and urinal as he pissed. He flushed and stepped before the sink, turning the dial of the faucet. Next, he got some of the pink soap foam in his palm and lathered his hands until they were masked white. He cupped his hands below it and filled his hands splashing it against his face twice. Gripping the sides of the porcelain sink, he stared into the mirror, which also had graffiti on it. Taking in his reflection, he took note of his features. Kreon was a young man, 27 years of age with an almond hue. He rocked a close fade with a thin goatee. He stood about five-foot-ten and weighed all of 260 pounds.

He wasn't a bad looking dude at all. In fact, some may say that he was fairly attractive. It didn't matter to him, though. Being attractive was the least of his concerns. He was struggling everyday with his mental instability. Ever since he was 11-years-old, he had been withdrawn and antisocial. He had low self-esteem and trouble maintaining relationships. It was mostly due to his moods changing so frequently. They would switch every few minutes or hours. On top of that, a lot of times he felt confused, not just about life but about himself in general. He had trouble distinguishing whether he was good or evil. He thought that he and other people were one or the other, there was no in between. He saw everything in either black or white. There weren't any gray areas for him.

"Kreon," he heard his therapist, Dr. Fonzworth, calling his name from the waiting room.

Quickly, he snatched a few paper towels from the dispenser and patted his face dry. Next, he dried off his hands and balled up the paper towels, tossing them in the trash can on the way out of the door. As soon as Kreon pushed open the door and stepped out onto the waiting room floor, he was greeted by the smile of a very tall man. He looked to be of mixed heritage; this was his therapist. Kreon had never asked him his ethnicity but, if he had to guess, he'd have to say that he was African American and Filipino. Anyway, the man had a crown of dark curls that always looked like they were wet. He had a youthful appearance, looking like he could have been anywhere from 25 to 30- years-old. He was fitted in a v-neck and khakis, which he wore high above his ankles and loafers. He didn't wear any socks with these shoes. Kreon believed his shoes were funky as a mothafucka. The thought alone, brought a slight smirk to his lips.

"Hey, Kreon, good to see you. I'm glad you could make it." Fonzworth extended his hand, and he shook it firmly. Kreon believed that his therapist was gay because his hand was as soft as a baby's ass and he didn't have much bass in his voice. It was those reasons, along with his attire, that had him convinced. It didn't matter to him though; straight, gay, orange, blue, or mothafucking republican, if you were cool people, then Kreon fucked with you. Straight up.

"I'm straight. How are you?" he replied, following the taller man down the corridor towards his office.

"I can't complain. Every day above ground is a good day, you know?" Fonzworth glanced at him as they continued their journey, a slight smile on his face. When he said this, Kreon gave him a look that changed his facial expression to a solemn one. The doctor knew Kreon almost as well as he knew himself, so he was well aware of the fact that he didn't want to be alive. In fact, the only reason he hadn't attempted suicide lately was because he came to the conclusion that killing himself would be cowardly, and he was far from a bitch. There wasn't a hoe bone in his entire body.

"Here's my office." Fonzworth opened the door to his office and allowed his patient in first. The room was small. It housed a desk, two chairs, an end table, and a lamp. There was one window and it was currently opened. A cool breeze occasionally blew in and disturbed the sheer white curtains. "Please have a seat." The good doctor extended his hand to the wicker chair. Kreon sat down. For the millionth time he'd been there, he looked around the office, taking in its décor. To him, it was made up like a cheap ass motel, a real cheap ass motel.

Fonzworth removed his hospital-issued beeper and sat it down on the desk top, before sitting down and crossing his long, scrawny legs. Once he picked up his glasses and slid them onto his face, he picked up a clipboard that a couple of documents were attached to. Kreon watched him attentively, wondering what the hell he was looking over. He was about to ask him, when he cleared his throat with a fist to his mouth.

"Kreon, you know those series of questions that I asked you the last time you were here?" he inquired, wearing a serious expression.

"Yeah. What about them?" His forehead crinkled as he waited for an answer.

"It's a questionnaire to determine your diagnosis. If you answer yes to five out of the nine questions, then you have what is called Borderline Personality Disorder."

"Borderline Personality Disorder? What is that? You tryna' tell me that I have split personalities?"

"No." He shook his head and sat the clipboard on the desk top. "Not split personalities exactly. But-"

"The last few doctors I had before you said I was bipolar. Now, you sitting here telling me that I'm more fucked up than I originally thought I was? Jesus fucking Christ!" he exclaimed as he looked up at the ceiling, addressing the Almighty. "What the fuck did I do? What the fuck did I do for you to sentence me to the life of a fucking nut case!" He looked back at the therapist, eyes moistening. "How did I... did I get this shit?" he asked, teary eyed.

Fonzworth took a deep breath and answered him, "It's hard to say exactly, but the disorder could be contributed to physical, mental, and sexual child abuse, losing a parent, or environmental circumstances. If I'm not mistaken, you said that you grew up in the ghetto, right? It could have been something that happened there that was too traumatic for your adolescent mind."

Tears jetted down Kreon's cheeks unevenly; his bottom lip quivered as he fidgeted with his fingers.

"Again, so what chu tellin' me is that I'm mo' fucked up than I original thought?" He looked away, teardrops slicking down his face. Throwing his head up, he talked to God, "Goddamn, man, ain't a young nigga been through enough? Fuck, fuck, fuck!" He punched himself in the head with both fists, head beginning to feel sore and bringing forth a headache. By this time, snot was trying to drip out of one of his nostrils. "I get so sick and tired of this shit. I swear to God, I wanna just lay the fuck down and die." He shook his head, placing his palms to his face.

"Kreon," Fonzworth began, placing his bony hand on his shoulder, "I'm sorry, but rest assured that I'm gonna do everything in my power to…"

Kreon's head snapped up; his face was wet and his eyes were red webbed. Suddenly, his eyebrows arched and wrinkles formed around the beginning of his nose.

"Fuck you. Fuck you, you faggot ass mothafucka. You haven't helped me do shit so far!" He leaped up out of his chair and hurled it at Fonzworth with all his might. The doctor dove out of the way, narrowly missing the flying chair. It deflected off the wall and landed on its side on the floor.

While Kreon was going ham tearing up the office and shit, Fonzworth was scrambling out of the room. He ran out into the hallway through the opened door, calling for help and motioning whomever in his direction. Two therapists came running into the office, panic in their eyes. Kreon took swings at them, but they wrestled him to the floor. They held down his arms and legs. He struggled against them, but his efforts were futile. "Why me? Whyyyy me? God, why did you make me this way? Tell me why did I deserve this?" he bawled, chest trembling. He made ugly expressions as tears drenched his face. His face was so wet, it looked like it had Vaseline on it. Soon after, Kreon stopped struggling against the men that held him down, all of which were breathing hard and had sweaty faces.

"Haa! Haa! Haa! Haa! I'm sorry, Kreon, I'm sorry. Haa! Haa! Haa!" Fonzworth told him, out of breath. His hair was a mess and his clothes were wrinkled, like he'd fallen asleep in them. With that said, Kreon dropped his head back against the carpeted floor, staring up at the ceiling. He was silent. He swallowed the spit in his throat and shut his eyelids.

"I'm sorry, God, whatever I did to be this way, I'm sorry! Please forgive me, please..." he shuddered, as more tears fell.

That night

Kreon was crying his eyes out and gripping the steering wheel while driving through the streets of South Central Los Angeles. The light posts and the stop lights shined in on him. The illumination flashed on and off his face, making the tears on his cheeks resemble diamonds. He gritted his teeth and smacked his hand upside of his head.

"Why me, huh? Why the fuck was I the one chosen to have to deal with this shit?" he hollered up at the ceiling, punching it rapidly until he was out of breath. "All I want is to be normal, to be a normal fucking person!" He sniffled, wiping his nose with the back of his fist. "I should just end it, I should just fucking end it! I don't know why the fuck I keep going on living, anyway. It ain't like anybody gives a fuck about me, dead or alive! Who would care? Who would care if I'm no longer here? No one! That's who!" He mashed the gas pedal to the floor and the Pontiac revved up, speeding through the streets. He was driving so fast, the yellow lines in the streets looked like blurs. His eyes were focused on the intersection. Determination and madness was written across his face. He was ready to die.

Vroom!

Kreon went flying through the intersection past a big ass Dodge Ram truck on some chrome 26 inch rims. He had almost hit the mothafucka, but he didn't even blink. He wasn't afraid of death, not one fucking bit. His recklessness proved this.

Beep! Beep! Beep!

The nigga in the SUV honked his horn, having almost been hit in the intersection.

"Fuck you! Fuck you! Fuck you!" Spittle flew from off his lips, as he held his middle finger out of the window. More tears slid down his face, flooding his cheeks and running over his lips. He licked them, tasting the saltiness. Quickly, his thoughts were snatched away from the situation and he focused his attention ahead. There weren't many cars out on the streets, so he was left alone. At this point, he felt like being reckless. He felt like ending it all. He wanted to leave this world and hopefully end up in a better place, a place of tranquility. His solace. He wanted to be in this place where no mental illnesses or violence existed. In this place, the weather was always sunny and the birds were always chirping. Everyone was friendly and a pleasure to be around. This was where Kreon wanted to be, and he wanted to be there now.

Kreon mashed the pedal to the floor, causing the red hand on the speedometer to spin around to the other side. Next, he shut his eyelids and slowly removed his hands from the steering wheel. Instantly, he was transported to that beautiful place of tranquility he constructed inside of his head. He saw himself as a little kid. He was five years old. He had a curly afro and was dressed in a Michael Jackson *Beat It* T-shirt. The warmth of the sun was beating on his back, and he was running like a track star through a field of colorful flowers. Although he was moving fast, his movements were slow motion through his eyes. A smile curled his young face and dimpled his cheeks. He was running towards the end of the field, where there was a cliff. Coming towards the end, he leaped into the air and wings sprouted from his back. He took off flying, soaring across the sky while smiling hard and looking around.

Beep! Beep! Beep! Beep!

"Watch where the fuck you're going!"

"What the hell is your problem?"

All the sounds from the outside slowly came flooding back to Kreon. His eyelids snapped open and he gasped when he looked up. A big ass Mack truck was heading directly at him. His Pontiac was about to collide with it, so he quickly swerved out of the way. His vehicle fishtailed and he struggled to get control of it, trying his best not to hit any oncoming cars. His whip's tires screeched and it finally came to a jerking stop. Kreon threw his ride in park and laid back in the seat, shutting his eyelids. He breathed heavily as his chest jumped wildly. His heart was beating madly, after having come so close to death. He made an ugly face as tears cascaded down his cheeks.

Kreon's mind was his prison.

CHAPTER THREE

"Yo, Nigel, lemme getta Rum and Coke, family." Kreon waved the bartender over. The slender, dark skinned man with the graying afro nodded to him as he fixed a patron's drink. As soon as he finished, he went on to make Kreon's drink of choice. The entire time that he was making the alcoholic beverage, he kept his eyes on him. He could tell that something was troubling the young man, but he couldn't quite put his finger on it. Being that he was a bartender, he also acted as a therapist of sorts to a host of his patrons. From his years of knowing the nigga before him, he knew off top that he wasn't the one to voice his problems. Nah, he was the type to bury his deep inside and deal with them as best as he could.

Once Nigel had finished making the drink, he sat a napkin, then sat his glass down on top of it. Kreon dropped a couple of bills down on the bar top and deposited his money back inside of his pocket. Nigel gave him a nod as he picked up the dead presidents, twiddling the toothpick at the corner of his mouth. Afterwards, he made his way down the opposite end of the bar to attend to another patron. Once Nigel had finished taking the patron's order, he went about the task of preparing it.

Kreon found himself staring down the bar at the sharply dressed older gentleman. He was brown skinned with a perfectly trimmed goatee and a haircut like Frank, Moesha's father in the tv show. The gent clipped off the end of his cigar with some kind of shiny gold mechanism, then used the flame of a lighter to light it while twisting the overgrown cigarette from side to side. He sucked on it twice and smoke came rushing out, polluting the air. Kreon caught a whiff of the cigar smoke and instantly thought about his late grandfather. He remembered there being a time that he smoked cigars, until he found out that he had heart disease and had to stop. By then, it was too late; the Lord had come knocking on his door to take him to a better place. At least that's what his mother had told him at the time. The thought of his grandfather brought tears to Kreon's eyes, but he blinked them back, dampening his eyelashes.

Flashback

When young Kreon entered his grandfather's room, he found his relatives surrounding his bed. All that could be heard was the weeping of the people that he shared blood with and constant rasping. Kreon slowly stepped forth, making his way through his kin, parting them like the Red Sea. His face was soaked with tears; he was constantly wiping his nose with the sleeve of his jacket. He found the 62-year-old man that he'd loved like he was his father, laid up in bed. The man had an unkempt salt and pepper afro and beard. His eyelids were narrowed into slits, but his eyes were red webbed and glassy. His thin lips trembled with every breath that he struggled to take. Just moments ago, he was unhooked from the machines that were meant to keep him alive. Now, he was situated to die slowly.

Miraculously, his wrinkled hand twitched. Kreon frowned, thinking that maybe he was calling out to him to take his hand. The grandson looked up to his grieving mother, who nudged him forth to say his last goodbye to his grandparent. Taking a deep breath but still crying, Kreon stepped before his grandfather, taking his hand into his own. Sniffling, he shut his eyelids briefly and pressed himself to say all that was on his mind.

"Grandfather, I'm scared. I'm really scared right now." He sniffled and wiped his nose with the back of his fist. "I don't want chu to die. You're... you're the only father I have, you can't leave me. Please, don't leave me..." he broke down crying and shuddering. Seeing the

14-year-old in such emotional pain caused more tears to slick the present adult's cheeks. Tears welled up in his grandfather's eyes and came sliding down his face as he breathed huskily. He wanted so badly to take his grandson into his arms and hold him, but the condition that he was in wouldn't allow it. He was a dying man and, shortly, his time would be coming to an end.

Kreon looked up at the ceiling, talking to God. "Please, God, don't take him away. I love him so much. I will do anything, Father. Anything you ask of me! Just please spare my grandfather." He looked to his grandfather and his eyelids were slowly beginning to shut; his breathing was growing weaker. This made him panic; he looked back up to the ceiling and stomped his foot on the linoleum repeatedly. "Please, please, please, God, no!" he bowed his head and whimpered. The rest of his family members whimpered as well. The women buried their tear-streaked faces into their husband and boyfriends' chests, as they looked on at the heartbreaking scene unfolding before their very eyes.

Kreon brought his soaked face up and snatched a couple of Kleenex from the box on the nightstand, blowing his nose. After he was done, he balled the tissue up and crawled into bed. He snuggled up next to his grandfather and pulled his arm around him, shutting his eyelids. "I remember everything that you ever taught me about being a man. I'll never forget any of it. I'ma be just like you when I grow up. I'ma marry me a beautiful woman, have kids, and work hard to provide and protect them..." His cheeks were coated with another set of tears and his bottom lip quivered. Sniffing back snot, he pressed on to finish what he had to say. "Thank you, Grandfather. Thank you for being the dad I never had. Thank you for loving me like your own. I'm going to miss you, I love you so much." He peeled his eyelids back open and more tears ran down his face. When he looked back up, his grandfather had just shut his eyelids and took his last breath. Seeing this, Kreon kissed him on the side of his head, then on the cheek. He laid there snuggled against him until he was forced to get up. Downstairs inside of the cafeteria, he cried long and hard in his mother's arms.

Present

Kreon wiped the moisture from his eyes with the sleeve of his jacket. He picked up his glass of alcohol, studying the dark liquor occupying it. He acknowledged that mixing the drugs he was on with the alcohol was a bad idea, but he needed something to suppress the demons he fought every day and night. Still, he didn't need to partake and wind up flipping out inside of the bar. The last thing he wanted to do was wake up with a hangover in jail. Taking a deep breath, Kreon sat the glass back down on the bar top and called the bartender over to order a cranberry juice. The old man obliged him and went on to clean off the bar top.

Kreon had just picked up his glass to take a sip when he saw a short, dark-skinned woman waltz in. She wore her individual braids pulled back in a bun and glasses decorated her face, loop earrings hung from her ears. She was hippie and had breasts the size of coconuts. She wasn't skinny, nor was she fat. To him, she was just the right size, especially for him. This young lady was wearing a short-sleeve plaid shirt, black leggings, and flip flops. Her curious eyes scanned the establishment, taking in all her surroundings. It was like she was looking for someone, but Kreon felt that he knew otherwise. To him, she was seeing if the bar was somewhere she wanted to take up time. If the place was too crowded, then she would be on her way. But if it was scarce of people, she'd help herself to a drink and music.

Kreon gathered that she had decided to stay for a while because she was headed in his direction, adjusting the strap of her purse on her shoulder. Seeing this, he focused his eyes back on his drink and indulged in it.

The dark-skinned woman sat down on the stool beside him and placed her purse on the bar top. She rummaged inside of her purse until she found an electric cigarette, and then she ordered a glass of Moscato. She was taking a few pulls from the end of the white device when the drink was sat before her on a napkin. She thanked the bartender, and he went on about his business.

The dark-skinned girl glanced at Kreon and then his drink; her brows furrowed. "Cranberry juice, huh?"

He glanced at the glass and looked at her, smirking, "Yep."

"Are you on your period?" She gave him a throaty laugh.

"Good one." He grinned, thinking that she was attractive. "You gotta cute laugh."

This caused her chocolate cheeks to turn red; she was blushing like a teenage girl being smitten by her high school crush. She chuckled with her hand over her mouth, trying not to show her teeth. Growing up, she had always thought that she looked like a little rabbit with her big front teeth.

"Thank... thank you," she snickered.

"You're welcome, beautiful." He gave her a dimpled smile. This caused her to blush further.

"Thanks again." She coughed on a bit of the smoke from the electric cigarette. No one had ever told her that she was beautiful before, especially not someone so handsome. Suddenly, a wide smile stretched across her full lips. Her top lip was dark, while the bottom one was pink. To Kreon, she had the most amazing smile that he had ever seen in his life.

"Is that smile for me?" He smiled, taking a sip of his cranberry juice.

"Oh, my God, will you stop?" She covered her entire mouth with her hand and smacked his hand.

"I'm only speaking on the real, sweetheart. I'ma always keep it a stack, if I don't do nothin' else." He shot her a dead serious expression. This made her clear her throat with her fist to her mouth and get serious as well.

"Nice to know." She went on to smoke on her electric cigarette, blowing out smoke in the air. Kreon and the dark-skinned girl, whom he discovered name was Odette, but he decided to call her O. Kreon and O laughed, conversed and drunk the remainder of the night away.

Kreon and Odette went on to chop it up the entire time they were at The Bar Fly. Before they knew it, time had passed them by and it was time to go.

***

Kreon and Odette left out of The Bar Fly holding hands, swinging their arms back and forth while staring into one another's eyes. The hefty young man leaned in to kiss the young lady, and she shut her eyelids and puckered up her lips. He bypassed her lips and kissed her on the cheek. He pulled back while smirking, and her brows furrowed with confusion.

Odette smiled and smacked him on his arm while saying, "Don't be trying to play me, boy. You better gimme my kiss."

Kreon chuckled and kissed her on the lips. "Them big, juicy thangs. Them plumpers." He kissed her again, slipping a little tongue inside of her mouth. Their heads slightly tilted in opposite directions as they kissed slow and passionately. When he pulled back, she appeared to be drunk off his kiss. She smiled and stared up at him like he was the fireworks exploding in the dark sky on the 4th of July.

"That was nice," she told him, smiling and wiping the spit at the corners of his mouth with her small hand.

Kreon took her hand and kissed the palm of it, keeping eye contact with her. He then interlocked his fingers with hers and kissed the back of her hand, bringing it down beside him. They walked down the street laughing and talking.

"Fresh, long stem roses folks! Get your fresh, long stem roses here!" an elderly man's voice came from behind them. They stopped and turned around. At the end of their line of vision, they found an old, white homeless man. He had ocean blue eyes and long, dirty blonde hair that spilled from beneath his tattered beanie. He was in a sweater, which he wore beneath a trench coat. His hands were in wool gloves, gripping the handle of a shopping cart. The old gent pushed the cart along and it rattled as it went down the sidewalk, rolling over cracks and small dips. The rattling of the cart disturbed the long-stemmed roses that were inside of the white buckets that harbored them.

Kreon stopped where he was looking back and forth between Odette and the homeless man pushing the shopping cart with the bucket of roses in them. He could tell by the expression on Odette's face that she wanted one of the roses. Acknowledging this, he grinned and told her to hold up. He approached the man with the roses. Odette watched, as he pulled a wad of wrinkled bills from out of his pocket and began counting them off. She observed Mr. Wonderful have a brief exchange with the roses merchant before passing him a few dollars.

"G lookin' out." Kreon touched fists with the cat that he'd purchased the roses from and headed back in the object of his affection's direction, smiling.

"Fresh, long stem roses folks! Get your fresh, long stem roses here!" the homeless man called out, trying to garner customers as he pushed the shopping cart along. He'd just crossed Kreon's path when he passed Odette the long stem rose that he'd bought for her.

"Here you go, slim." Kreon watched as little momma took the rose. She shut her eyelids and brought the flower to her nose, inhaling deeply. Her lips stretched across her face and curled at their ends, showcasing that enchanting smile of hers.

"Oh, Kreon, it smells wonderful." She took the rose from her nose and looked at it. She then brought it back to her nose and inhaled its essence once again. Little momma absolutely loved that he'd copped it for her.

"Oh, really? Well, plant one here." He tapped his cheek. She leaned forward and he turned his head toward her, his lips intercepting hers. Odette blushed and smiled, looking like a smitten teenage girl.

"That was slick, real slick." She pointed and smiled once again. "Sooo, uuhhh, are you a gangbanger?"

He chuckled and said, "Nah, I ain't no gangbanger, girl.

Odette took in his attire before replying, "Well, you look the part."

Kreon was in a plaid shirt, Dickie shorts, and socks pulled up to his knees and low-top Chuck Taylor Converse. Homie was looking like a real L.A. gang member.

He gave himself the once over and said, "I'ma product of my environment, sweetheart, but nah. A nigga ain't flaggin'. Shit, every nigga from Killa Cali ain't a banga."

"So, what are you then, a gangster? A thug?"

He shrugged and said, "Kreon, is Kreon."

"I hear you, sir."

"I thought that you would. This yo' raggedy ass Civic?" he asked her, as they came upon a turquoise Honda Civic.

She laughed and said, "Fuck you! Don't be talking about my car, punk!"

Odette stepped to her car and unlocked the driver side door. Kreon looked out for her as he held the door open for her to get inside. Once she had ducked inside, he slammed the door shut and ducked down inside of the window.

"You all set, lil' momma?"

"Yeah." She smiled, batting her eyelashes. She thought he was finer than a mothafucka and was trying to win him over.

"Alright then, take it easy." He patted the roof of her whip and started off in the opposite direction, hands inside of his pockets. He spat on the sidewalk and kept it moving, leaving a frown on her face. She was expecting him to ask for her number, but he didn't.

"Hold up. Wait a minute, aren't chu gonna ask me for my number?" she called out of the driver side window, watching his back as he walked down the street.

"Nope," he smirked, with his head tilted back.

"I had a great time; I would like to see you again."

"Okay," he replied, still walking.

"Well, are you gonna gimme yo' number or what?"

"Sure. Why not?"

Hurriedly, Odette grabbed a napkin from out of the glove box and took an ink pen from out of the change tray. Pulling the cap off the ink pen with her teeth, she called out of the window for the charming young man's number. She jotted it down on the napkin, as he hollered out the digits.

"...8997!"

"Okay. I'm going to call you."

Kreon didn't say anything. He threw up two fingers and kept it moving towards his car.

Odette stared at him through the sideview mirror until he'd disappeared. Smiling, she held the napkin in both hands and stared at it. She then kissed it and held it to her chest, looking up at the ceiling. Next, she took a deep breath and looked at the digits scrolled on the napkin again. Her eyes darted to their corners as she thought about something. That's when she folded up the napkin and placed it inside of her purse. Setting her purse aside on the passenger seat, she leaned over the steering wheel and peered up through the windshield at the sky. Above, she saw a full moon and stars scattered around it.

"Lord... hey... hi, it's me again, Odette." She shut her eyelids briefly and swallowed the spit in her throat. "I don't know if you remember me or not but, a while ago, I came to you, asking that you send me a good man. Well, I really, really like this one and before I go fantasizing about our future together. You know, the girly stuff that we women do when we think we've met 'The One'?" she curled and uncurled the two fingers on both of her hands.

"Seriously though, before I go overthinking things with this dude, let me know if he's the one. I mean, I don't expect for you to start talking or nothing. I mean, unless you decide to use another human being as a vessel or something. Oh, please, don't do that because I'd die. Some supernatural stuff like that wouldn't do anything but give my little butt a heart attack. Okay, listen, I'll settle for a sign in any form that you choose. Just give me something that lets me know that I'm not wasting my time with Mr. Kreon and that I should give him a call."

She took the time to take a deep breath and then said, "Okay. Lord, is Kreon the man that you sent for me?" She took in her surroundings, looking for any sign to clarify that Mr. Wonderful from The Bar Fly was her guy, but she didn't get anything. Finally, she looked up at the sky, staring up at it unblinkingly. Suddenly, one of the stars twinkled. This made her smile and bounce up and down in her seat, clapping her hands. She was genuinely excited about the new man in her life and she couldn't wait to hear his voice again.

CHAPTER FOUR
Later that night

Once Kreon made it down to the end of the hallway to the chipped green apartment door marked with the fading number 15, he knocked and stuck his hand back inside of his hoodie, looking about to see if anyone was watching him.

"Who is it?" he heard his uncle's voice boom from the opposite side.

"It's Kre, Unc!" he hollered back.

"Hold on, man," he heard his uncle again. A couple of seconds later, he was undoing the locks and pulling the door open. Kreon crossed the threshold and his uncle, Omar, shut the door behind him. He made sure to lock all the locks that aligned the door before turning around to his nephew. "What's up, boy?" He dapped him up with a latex gloved hand.

"Ain't much, just slid through here tryna get right."

"Is that right? Where yo' momma at?" He stepped back to the stove, where he was whipping cocaine into crack. Omar was a husky man of a caramel hue. His hair was parted into six neat cornrows that just reached his neck. A thick goatee aligned his chubby face and mouth. He had a hairy chest and a round belly. Red Dickie's hung slightly off his ass and put some of his butt crack on display.

Omar was a man that loved fast cars and fast women. He knew that the only way to keep these things, he had to have money, lots of money, which was why he'd been slinging drugs since he was 12-years-old. At first, he was nickel and dime hustling; eventually, he graduated from ounces and then to bricks. He hustled crack, weed, and X-pills. He was the neighborhood dopeman, the nigga you needed to see if you wanted some work at a decent price.

"At home, I guess. I haven't gone back to the crib yet. I was down at The Bar Fly, gettin' my mind right."

"Is that right? Was ol' Nigel down there tonight?"

"Yeah, he was there." Kreon pulled out a small knot of money and began counting off the bills he'd need to purchase the illegal goods.

"That's a good dude…"

"What's up, fat boy?" Jaekwon came walking into the kitchen with his arm in a cast. He was a tall, skinny light skinned nigga that resembled the rapper T.I. RTBG was tattooed in red ink below his right eye. He sported a receding hairline and a shadow fade. His goatee was barely visible, looking like the whiskers of a cat more than a man's facial hair. At the moment, he was dressed in a Falcon's fitted cap, which he wore backwards and cocked to the side. His black T-shirt fitted him perfectly and his camouflage cargo pants hung off his waist, showcasing his red canvas belt. The belt's buckle had the number '20' engraved on it.

"Sup, nigga?" Kreon smacked the dead presidents on the counter top beside his uncle. He then slapped hands with his cousin and embraced him, patting him on the back. Breaking their embrace, he looked to the cast on his relative's arm and his forehead wrinkled. "Fuck happened to yo' arm?"

"Mannnn, a nigga slipped and fell on a wet floor at Superior Market over there off Slauson. I busted my ass and broke my arm. You know I'ma 'bouta sue the dog shit outta them fools. Tell me that's notta big ass mothafuckin' lawsuit, Blood." He shook his head and inattentively rubbed his cast, which several of his homeboys had autographed.

"The biggest lawsuit," Kreon stated.

"You just make sure you break me offa chunk of whatever you get outta them crackas," Omar said, still whipping up the drugs.

"Two sho'. I'ma break the whole family off. You know how we do," Jaekwon assured him.

"That's what's up." Kreon nodded.

"I'm thirsty as a mothafucka, what chu got up in here?" Jaekwon asked, opening the refrigerator and grabbing a bottle of Aquafina. "I'm finna get up outta here, man." He slapped hands with his cousin and uncle. "Unc, good lookin' on the pills; that's love." He was talking about the Mollies that let him have on the love. He had a new bitch on the line that was into popping pills. He'd hit up a few of the homies hoping that they'd have some, but there wasn't anybody holding, so he hollered at his uncle.

Omar gave Jaekwon a nod and he left. Kreon shut the door behind him. "Now, what was you saying earlier about Nigel, Unc?" Kreon came walking back inside of the kitchen from the door.

"Oh, Nigel. Yeah, OG has been my therapist many, many, many nights. He knows some secrets of mine."

Kreon's forehead crinkled and he said, "You trust that old ass nigga with yo' personal business?"

He nodded and responded, "I know some secrets of his. It's a give and a take."

"I griff you." (Which meant, I feel you)

"Anyway, what chu want? Yo' usual?" he asked with his back to him, holding up a jar with murky water in it. The glass was fogged and he was swirling it around, eyes focused on the white substance at the bottom of it. It was in the beginning of its hardening stage.

Sitting there watching his uncle, Kreon thought back to the time he first copped from him. He gave the young nigga a hustle and he'd always be grateful for it. It was because of him that he could eat.

Flashback

Kreon sat at the scarred-up wooden table inside of the kitchen in the trap. He was slumped over in his chair with his hands nestled in his lap; his head on a swivel. While he was busy looking around, Omar was doing something in his bedroom. His shadow was casted on the hallway wall as he was handling a task. Shortly thereafter, the OG came strolling from out of the bedroom with a wrinkled brown paper bag in his hand. He pulled out a chair and planted himself in it, his gold Rolex chain dangling around his neck. Staring his nephew dead in his eyes, he took a deep breath. Afterwards, he searched his eyes for any uncertainty, but he didn't find any. As far as he could tell, his blood was ready to jump into the water head first.

"Kreon." Omar knocked on the table top to garner his nephew's attention. Once he had it, he made sure that they held eye contact. He wanted to make sure that he understood everything that he was about to run down to him. "In this bag is some very illegal shit. Shit that yo' mothafuckin' ass can get locked up for. You about to cross over to the other side. The criminal element, my nigga. Once you take this, you signin' an imaginary contract that says you gon' stay loyal to this game and neva' rat, under any circumstances. You feel me?" Kreon nodded. "Alright, if you take this shit, you didn't get it from me. You understand?" He raised his eyebrows.

"I gotchu, Unc, damn." he stated, annoyed. His uncle lowered the bag within his reaching distance and he snatched it away, looking inside of the wrinkled bag. He cracked half of a smile, being pleased with what he saw before his eyes. He rolled the bag up and stashed it inside of his leather jacket. Standing to his feet, he pulled out the crinkled, dead white men, as his uncle rounded the table. The OG took the money and didn't bother to count it. He

gave his nephew a manly embrace, patted him on the back, then kissed him on the cheek.

"I love you." He patted him on the cheek like an old, Italian wise guy.

"I love you, too." Kreon stared at the money he'd given him in his hand. "Ain't chu gon' count that?"

"Do I need to?" He raised an eyebrow.

"Hell naw." He frowned, scrunching up his nose. "I keep it a hunnit alla time."

"Fa sho'." Omar dapped him up and smiled. He then unlocked the door and pulled it open, stepping aside so that his kin could leave. As soon as his nephew crossed the threshold, he called him back. The young man looked over his shoulder. "The streets ain't for everybody, that's why they made sidewalks."

Kreon nodded and went on about his business.

Present

"Yep. Same old, same old," Kreon responded to his uncle. Hearing someone laughing, he looked over his shoulder to find someone inside of the compact living room. The lights were out and the blue illumination from the television screen was flickering off the person's face. Narrowing his eyes and peering closely, he realized that it was Candy's thick, yellow ass. She was lying across the couch, swirling her finger around one of her individual braids. Her eyes were focused on the tv and she had a crooked smile on her face, like she was about to laugh at something at any given moment. Her tattooed wrist, which bore his uncle's name, dangled off the edge of the couch, while her hand held the remote control of the 55-inch Vizio flat-screen.

Candy was a young lady half Omar's age. She had an hourglass shape, juicy thighs, an ass, and a pair of tits that wouldn't quit. The two of them had met at his homeboy's daughter's 16th birthday party. She had been best friends with the B-day girl since elementary school. Although she was young, she was really developed for someone her age, which was why she had so many niggaz at the party drooling over her, Omar's thirsty ass included. Seeing niggaz already plotting, the OG knew he had to make his move fast before the young lady had on her choosing shoes.

Omar was much older than Candy, so he didn't have to press her that hard. Candy had daddy issues; being a master of manipulation, he played on that and eventually had her eating out of the palm of his hand. He taught her how to suck, fuck, and do all the freaky shit he liked so much. In addition to that, he had her holding guns and transporting drugs for him. He molded her into the bitch that every hustler needed and he was damn proud of it. She was one of the many girls that he had in pocket, and she knew this. Homegirl was alright with that; she felt that she was a forerunner for being wifey. She only hoped that, soon, *her* man would see how down for him that she was and sit her in a throne right beside his own.

"Alright." Omar finished up with the coke he was cooking and pulled off his latex gloves, discarding them inside of the trashcan. He went off to retrieve what his nephew wanted. A minute later, he returned with a wrinkled brown paper bag, sitting it in his sister's son's lap. Kreon opened the bag and was pleased with what he saw inside. He nodded his satisfaction and rolled the bag back up. Rising to his feet, he stuffed the bag down in front of his Dickie's and slapped hands with his uncle, who kissed him on the cheek and patted him on his back.

"Remember…" He pointed his finger in his face and waited for him to finish what he was saying.

"If I get caught with this shit, I don't know you," he repeated what he'd told him every time he bought drugs off him.

"Smart nigga." He smiled, squeezing the back of his neck affectionately while kissing the side of his head. Although Kreon didn't come from his nut sack, he still looked at him like he was his son. Therefore, he was trying to mold him in his image. At first, he didn't agree with him getting involved with the street life but, seeing as how he wasn't going to stay away, he decided to take him under his arm and school him to the game.

"Alright."

Omar looked to Candy and told her to say goodbye to his nephew. She stopped curling her hair around her finger and looked to Kreon, grinning and waving. "Bye, Kreon."

"See you later, Candy," he responded then turned to his uncle. "Anyway, Unc, I'ma gon' get up outta here."

"Alright, man." He unchained and unlocked the door, pulling it open. "Hit me up and let me know you got in safe."

"Fa sho'." He dapped him up and took his leave.

Tranay Adams

CHAPTER FIVE

Jaekwon bopped off to his Infinity truck while whistling. Once he was finally at the driver's door of the SUV, he looked around to make sure no one was watching as he pulled out his Beretta. Next, he unlocked the door. He'd just placed his hand on the vehicle's handle, when a Crown Victoria screeched to a halt beside him. The backdoor swung open and a reddish-orange haired man in a cheap ass suit hopped out.

"Gimme that fucking gun." The man snatched the Beretta from out of his hand and grabbed him by the back of his neck, squeezing it tightly. The pressure of his steel-grip caused Jaekwon to grimace, as he was swung around and forced into the backseat of the car. The reddish-orange haired man took a cautious look around before switching hands with the Beretta and hopping into the backseat. He slammed the door shut behind him and gave the driver the signal to drive off.

Jaekwon sat quietly in the backseat, wondering where he was being taken. When he looked up front to the driver, all he could see was his bald, shiny head. Bald head adjusted the rearview mirror and looked up at Jaekwon through his reflection, his menacing eyes on display. Jaekwon held eye contact with him for a minute, before looking over at the white nigga that had thrown his black ass into the backseat of the car. He was staring ahead with a not-so-friendly look on his face. In fact, neither of these mothafuckas seemed to be happy whenever he saw them. Hell, you would think that he'd done something to them, but he hadn't so much as given them a dirty look.

The bald head mothafucka behind the wheel was Detective Burton and the mean son of a bitch with the reddish-orange hair sitting beside him was Detective Bland.

Without saying a word, Bland lifted Jaekwon's shirt up and ripped off the wire that was taped down to his chest, taking some of his chest hair with it. The thug grimaced, feeling the sting from the tape being ripped from off his chest. He laid back against the seat and rubbed the red bruising on his chest from the tape being ripped from off him.

Bland checked the tape, smiling once he heard some incriminating events against the asshole that they wanted bad. Afterwards, he wrapped the wire around the device that held the tape and stashed it inside of his suit's jacket.

"Good job, bitch, really good job." Bland patted Jaekwon on the cheek and then pinched it like a grandmother would. "We're building quite the case against that scumbag of an uncle."

"Is that enough, man? I mean, how much more do y'all need?" Jaekwon looked between the two detectives, forehead wrinkled.

"Don't ask me any fucking questions!" Bland growled and grabbed Jaekwon's inner thigh, applying pressure. He mad-dogged his confidential informant, seeing the pain his face while tears ran from out of the corners of his eyes. "I ask the questions here. Me and no one else, got it?"

"Yeah. I got it! I got it, man!" Jaekwon gritted his teeth.

"Good." Bland released his thigh and adjusted his tie.

"You got us some info that we could do some damage with, but it's not enough. Your uncle is looking at a conspiracy charge at best," Burton told Jaekwon, looking back and forth between his cousin and the windshield. "That's not what we want. We want enough evidence to bring his entire organization down, you got that?"

"Yeah, yeah, yeah," A grimacing Jaekwon rubbed his sore thigh. "I got it, I got it! You want enough evidence to bring him down... forever." He dropped his head back against the headrest of the backseat, thinking back to how he'd landed himself in this position.

Vrooooom!

A white Infinity truck blew up the street, leaving debris in its wake and crossing the intersection just as the stop light turned red. Jaekwon was behind the wheel, shoveling cocaine up his nose and listening to Ice Cube's 'Rhymes like weight'. The rap music was banging so hard inside of his SUV that it had that mothafucka pulsating, black tinted windows rattling.

I got lyrics that wake up spirits
They told me how to make big hits and spend digits
Can you dig it?
You fed, you dead, see red
My lead, yo head, I fed
Like you shit
I got rhymes push that shit like weight
My nigga Lincoln help me navigate
Through this hate retaliate, it's official
I got that bomb, bomb, diddy, diddy, diddy, bomb, bomb
When I hit you...

Jaekwon held the steering wheel with one hand while he quickly snorted the line of coke from off his fist. The potent drug stabbed at his brain like the dull tip of a needle, turning his eyes glassy and causing his throat to drip. He blinked his eyelids continuously and swept his thumb across his nose, snorting like a big ass hog. When he threw his head back, he saw his eyes in the rearview mirror. The nigga looked high as a mothafucka, but he didn't care because that powder seemed to always get his mind right.

Jaekwon licked the cocaine residue off his fist and threw his head back, snorted again. He ran his hand down his face and started bobbing his head to the beat of the music, looking around and shit. He began screaming louder and louder, veins bulging at his temples and neck. Looking around, he began to spit the lyrics along with Ice Cube. Casually, he glanced up into the rearview mirror and saw the red and blue flashing lights of a police car. He said "Oh, shit," and his eyelids stretched wide open. The sudden appearance of the law sobered that ass up quick, fast, and in a hurry. See, not only was this stupid mothafucka driving over the speed limit, he had a loaded gun wedged between the console and driver seat. Not only that, he had two kilos of cocaine in the hatch of his truck.

"Stupid! Stupid! Stupid!" Jaekwon punched himself in the side of his head repeatedly. A confused expression crossed his face, as he tried to think of what he should do next. Coming up with what he thought was the best action, he snatched his Beretta from where it was wedged. "Fuck that shit, blood! I'm not going jail!" Using the hand that held his gun, he wiped his dripping nose, blinking his eyelids repeatedly. He licked his lips and glanced up into the rearview mirror again, adjusting it quickly.

Afterwards, he cranked up the volume of the Ice Cube track and snorted some more coke, preparing himself to go gun to gun with the pig that was about to pull him over. He bobbed his head hard, gassing himself up for the confrontation. Once he figured that he was good to go, he pulled over to the side of the street and let his window down, seeing the cop hop out of his ride and advance in his direction. Anxious, Jaekwon hopped out his truck and ran off, taking shot after shot at the cop.

Bloc! Bloc! Bloc!

The first two shots went wild, but the third one struck the cop in the bulletproof vest which he wore underneath his uniform, knocking him off his booted feet. Jaekwon was about to lower his weapon, when headlights from behind stole his attention. When he whipped around, he was blinded by the headlights of a 2004 bluish-green Ford

Focus. The horn of the small vehicle blared and it came to a screeching halt, slamming into Jaekwon. His eyes stretched wide open and his mouth fell open, just as the car collided with him. The impact sent him tumbling over the side of the vehicle and landing hard on his arm, breaking it. His .9mm landed two feet away from him. He laid where he was clutching his wounded limb and hollering in agony. Before he knew it, the cop came upon him wincing and clutching his gun with both hands, ready to give him some shit that would leave him lying still forever.

"Move and I'll blow your fuckin' brains out!" the cop warned him, then responded to the dispatcher on his radio.

As soon as the handcuffs were clamped on Jaekwon's wrists, he was talking about making a deal. The sniveling son of a bitch couldn't wait to spill his guts. He was singing like Gladys Knight on his way down to the precinct. The cops couldn't get him to shut the fuck up, so they just listened without saying a word.

As much as Jaekwon had hustled and done dirt in the streets, he'd never caught a case. That would have been his first time on lock, doing a bid. He'd heard a lot of horror stories from his homies about being in prison and he was willing to do anything that would ensure that he didn't have to go.

Jaekwon cut a deal, agreeing to be an informant. They wanted his uncle Omar badly. But, they didn't have anything on him. The Boys agreed to grant Jaekwon's bitch ass full immunity, if he brought them enough evidence to bury his uncle alive. With the deal made, Jaekwon was fitted with a wire.

"That's a good, bitch, you were listening," Burton said, of Jaekwon's understanding that they wanted enough evidence to bring Omar's entire organization down. The spiteful detective looked back and forth between the rearview mirror and Jaekwon. He and his partner didn't have any problem with disrespecting their informant. The way they saw it, he'd better take whatever treatment they dished out at him, or he'd be looking at a long stay in the federal penitentiary.

Jaekwon shook his head and placed his hand over his face, shaking his head sadly. Taking his palm away from his face, he said, "What the fuck am I doin'? Man, this shit is foul, this shit is fucked up! I'm on some slimeball shit, settin' my peeps up to get knocked off." He looked up at the ceiling of the vehicle and blew out his frustration, cheeks swelling up. "Yo' Bland, man, I can't do this anymore, fam. I can't even stand to look at my reflection in the mirror." He told him this while looking him square in his eyes.

Bland's eyebrows sloped and he twisted his lips up. "Fuck you and your honorary code of the streets! You already started down this road and I say you're gonna finish traveling down it. Now, you listen up and you listen good. It's either this or a very fucking long stretch in the feds. It's all on you, my nigga. Make your choice, Blood!" He looked at him with flaring nostrils and a tight lip, waiting for his decision.

"Fuck it, man." Jaekwon threw up his hand. "Like you said, I already started down this road, so I may as well keep strollin' down the mothafucka, ya griff me?"

"Yeah, whatever the fuck that means. Now, just to show you that I and my charming partner here aren't just a couple of mean motor scooters, we brought you a little present." Bland reached down between his legs on the floor and came back up with a jewelry box. Sitting it on his lap, he removed the lid. Inside, there was an icy gold chain with a tiger head medallion. It had rubies for eyes, pink diamonds for its tongue, and black diamonds for its mouth. The ferocious animal was roaring. "Here you go. Ain't she a beaut?" A smiling Bland looked back and forth between the chain and Jaekwon's surprised expression. The thug held the box that the jewelry was in, its diamonds twinkling from the light illuminating it through the vehicle's windshield.

"Y'all for real? This chain is really for me?" Jaekwon asked the detectives.

"That's what the fuck he said, didn't he?" Burton scowled from the driver's seat. He mean-mugged the thug through the rearview mirror once again. He didn't respect or like Jaekwon. It wasn't because he was a criminal. Nah, that wasn't it at all. He hated him because he was a street nigga with a code, 'No Snitching', but he didn't abide by it. Had he'd been a standup nigga, he and his partner would have treated him with respect. But, he wasn't, so that's why they consistently referred to him as Bitch and not his government name. The way they saw it, they were his pimps and he was their whore. The only difference being was that they put him out on the streets to collect information, instead of money.

"Ain't no need to be rude," Jaekwon told him, scowling back while still holding the jewelry box.

"I'll be whatever the fuck I want to, bitch. I'll advise you to watch your mouth, before I pull this motherfucker over and beat your young ass out in the middle of the street."

"Whatever, man," Jaekwon blew out his frustration and looked down at the chain. He smiled while looking at the beautiful piece, ready to put it on that minute. *This mothafucka hard, Blood. I gotta Roley I can rock this mothafucka with!* "May I?" he asked Bland of his wearing the chain.

"You like it?" Bland asked him, smirking.

"Like it? I love it," he exclaimed.

All this chain gone be is a reminder of what I done to get it. I'm 'pose to be a G with it, but here I am lettin' these cracka ass crackas turn me into a rat. Fuck it! The first rule of life is self-preservation. I gotta do what I gotta do.

Jaekwon shrugged and adjusted the chain hanging from his neck, admiring its craftsmanship and the clarity of the diamonds in it.

"Here we are," Bland announced, as they pulled up a few cars in front of the thug's Infinity truck.

"Alright. I'm out." Jaekwon held up his fist to give Bland dap, but he looked at it like it was covered in maggots. The thug dropped his hand and opened the car's door, stepping out. Slamming the vehicle's door, he walked around it and stepped upon the curb. He was about to make his way towards his truck when Bland called him back. When he turned around, he found the detective sitting up front with Burton, face visible in the window. He motioned Jaekwon over. The thug looked up and down the block to make sure that there wasn't anyone watching him, before he proceeded over to him. "What's brackin'?" he asked as he stooped low inside of the window, coming eye level of the detective.

"You forgot something." Bland handed him his Beretta and he took it, tucking it at the small of his back. "Oh yeah, one more thing." He motioned for him to stoop down again and whispered something into his ear. The news that he got etched a depressed expression across his face. The detected chuckled along with his partner and patted him on the shoulder. Afterwards, the Crown Victoria drove off down the block. Bland, peering into the sideview mirror, adjusted it and watched as a disappointed looking Jaekwon stood out on the block, growing smaller and smaller the further the Crown Victoria got from the scenery.

"Little dumb motherfucker," A grinning Burton shook his head shamefully. "You see his face? Beige bastard wasn't expecting that."

Bland suddenly grew serious, having come down from his laughter. "He better expect to spend the rest of life behind bars if he doesn't do like I told him."

"You don't think he will?" Burton looked back and forth between his partner and the windshield.

"I have faith that he will, but I'm just saying."

***

Jaekwon pulled open the door of his truck and whipped out his gun, sliding in behind the wheel. Slamming the door shut, he looked down at his chain and its diamonds twinkled. He then put down the sun-visor so that he could see his reflection, coming in contact with his eyebrows, eyes, and nose in the rectangle mirror.

"What the fuck? How I let myself get in bed with these mothafuckin' federal agents, Blood? I fucked up; I really, really fucked up this go around." His brows furrowed and his eyes misted with tears. He took the safety off his Beretta and revealed the red dot on the lethal weapon. He then opened his mouth and stuck the gun inside of it, his teeth biting down on the hard, black metal. Tears flew down his cheeks. He breathed heavily, taking deep breaths to work himself up to do the unthinkable. His shoulders rose and fell as his chest inflated and deflated. His nostrils flared and the small hairs in them moved animatedly from the hot air passing through them. Before long, there were green snot bubbles forming out of his nasal cavities.

"Aaarrrrrr! Aaarrrrr!" He pumped and pumped himself up, finger adding pressure to the trigger of his Beretta. He was getting dangerously close to blowing the top of his skull off. "Aaah!" He snatched his gun out of his mouth, looking around and rubbing the palm of his hand on the side of his head. Tears flowed down his cheeks and dripped off his chin. "I can't... I can't do it... I just can't." He laid his head back against the headrest and laid his Beretta on his lap, finger still on the trigger. He shut his eyelids and took a deep breath, throat going up and down his neck. He sat up like this for a minute before sitting back and sliding his weapon underneath the seat. Next, he stuck the key inside of the ignition and cranked it up. The beast came to life and he pulled off.

CHAPTER SEVEN

Shonda sat on the couch with her cordless telephone cradled to her ear by her shoulder. Her foot was propped up on the edge of the coffee table and she was painting her toenails red. At the time, she was dressed in leggings and gossiping on the jack with her homegirl, Asia. Marquise was sitting on the floor Indian-style watching his favorite cartoon, Paw Patrol.

"Bitch, you are fucking lying to me right now. No, that nigga didn't." A surprised look came over her face and she stabbed the tiny brush into the small glass jar of toenail polish. She was shocked to hear the news that her friend delivered. "You know what? I'm not even surprised that Melvin's ass likes dick. I told you I caught 'em looking at that flaming cashier at Walmart, like he wanted a piece of his lil' ass. When I brought up my suspicions to Jessica, her apple head ass swore before God Almighty that her man only entertains pussy. Ol' nasty ass nigga."

She shook her head shamefully and jumped to her feet, careful not to let her wet toes touch the carpet. She carried her five-foot, seven-inch form inside of the kitchen and opened the refrigerator, hunching over while searching its insides. Shonda listened to her big mouth friend run her mouth in her ear while she rummaged through the items. Grabbing a Pepsi, she popped the lid and kicked the refrigerator door shut behind her. Adjusting the cordless on her shoulder, she headed back inside of the living room. She was about to sit down, when a knock at the door stole her attention.

"Hold on, boo, let me see who this is at the door." Having sat the cordless down on the coffee table, she walked over to the door and glanced through the peephole. Confirming who it was on the opposite side, she unlocked all the locks and pulled the door open. As soon as she did, her little sister, Odette, came dancing over the threshold. A smile was plastered across her face and she was spinning around like a ballerina, inhaling the scent of the rose that Kreon had given her. Her big sister's face balled up and she looked at her strangely. She told her homegirl she'd talk to her later because she had a guest, but she was still bumping her gums when she was hanging up the telephone.

"Bitch, what the fuck are you so happy about?" Shonda asked, hand on her hip as she switched her weight from one foot to another.

Odette was just about to respond when her cellphone rang. Switching hands with the rose, she fished inside of her purse until she recovered her cellular. Seeing her mother's face and name on the screen, she rolled her eyes and ignored the call. Dropping her cellphone back inside of her purse, she looked back up at her sister. Again, she was about to answer her question until another distraction came.

"Mommyyyyyyy!" Marquise jumped up to his feet, running towards his mother. She grabbed him up and spun him around and around. The little boy laughed and giggled like he was being tickled by a pair of hands. A crooked smile came across his lips and his eyes rolled to their corners, head bobbing about. "Whoa! Whoa! Whoa! Mommy, I'm getting dizzy."

"Oh, I'm sorry, baby." Odette kissed her baby boy on the forehead and sat him down. They both wobbled about in a daze with silly looks on their faces. Eventually, Marquise fell out on the floor, staring up at the ceiling while smiling.

"Okay. Let's try this again, bitch; fuck is you so happy about?" Shonda placed her hand on hip and took a sip of her Pepsi, as she studied her sister's weird behavior.

"Oh, sister, my darling sister." Odette stuck her rose in her hair and danced over to her sibling. She took her Pepsi and set it aside. She then took her hands and danced around the living room with her. Marquise sat where he was, smiling. He was happy to see his mother so excited. "I met the most wonderful guy tonight."

"Oh, really? He dicked you down, huh?" Shonda quipped.

"Nope. But our convo' was off the chain," she said as she smiled delightfully, throwing her head back and clapping her hands.

Shonda took the time to spark up a blunt and blow smoke. "So, tell me, baby sis, what's this Mr. Wonderful like?"

"Oh my God, Shonda. He's handsome, intelligent, charming, and funny." Odette ducked off inside of the kitchen to the refrigerator and got what she wanted to out of it. She took a quick sip from her cup of Canada Dry ginger ale before continuing about 'Mr. Wonderful'. "He's nothing like any guy that I have ever met. He's so different from Carlos, Roderick, and Donnie."

"You're rambling on and on about Mr. Wonderful, but you've yet to give a sister his gov."

"Kreon," she spat. "Kreon Williams. I can see it now, Mr. and Mrs. Kreon Williams." She looked ahead while smiling, seeing her and Kreon walking down the aisle during their wedding. Although she had just met the young man, she had already envisioned a life with him. She wanted to wear his last name, bear his children, and go out on family getaways with him. It was safe to say that Kreon was her quote, unquote, *Dream Guy.*

"That nigga musta been shooting some hell of a good G at chu, Missy. 'Cause he definitely got chu wrapped around his finger." She plopped down on the couch and continued to partake in her bleezy, blowing smoke into the air.

"Whatever, bitch, let me finish telling you about my new boo thang." Odette plopped down on the couch beside her big sister.

Shonda leaned forth and dumped ashes from her blunt out into a glass ashtray. She then sat back on the couch and continued to take pulls from it, smoke wafting all around her. "I'm listening, gimme the rundown."

"Okay." A smiling Odette adjusted herself on the couch and told her sister what little she knew about Kreon. From what she had told her sister, she was starting to believe that she had met what she deemed the Perfect Guy.

***

"Grrrrrr," Kreon gritted hard, squeezing his eyelids shut. His fists were clenched so tightly that the veins were bulging through them. He was standing before the medicine cabinet mirror inside of the bathroom. The veins at his temples and the sides of his neck pulsated. He was dressed in an undershirt and gray sweatpants. Tears came bursting through his eyes and treading down his cheeks. "No! Noo! Nooo! Noooo!" He broke down sobbing, dropping his head with snot bubbling out of his left nostril. He looked back up at his reflection and saw that his entire face was so wet from his tears that it looked like he was sweating. "I'm not... weak... and I'll never give in. Do you hear me? I'll never give innnnn! Ah! Haa! Haa! Haa! Haa!" His entire form quivered and he gritted that much harder, dropping to his knees. He clenched his fists tighter and fell over onto his side, hugging his form. He curled up like a baby in a fetal position.

"I'm not weak... I'm notta punk! I'm notta goddamn coward! You're the fucking coward! You hear me? Huh?" Slowly, he got up on his hands and knees, teardrops falling from his eyes and splashing on the tiled floor. More snot bubbled out of his nostril, threatening to drip. "I'ma warrior, mothafucka! A mothafucking warrior, goddamn it! I didn't come this far just to lay down and die! I was given..."

He snorted back some of the snot and swallowed the spit that had accumulated in his throat. He sobbed louder and harder, trying his hardest to suppress the illness that coated his brain. Every single fucking day, he woke up depressed and wanting to die. He felt useless and hopeless. He felt like he couldn't do anything right, that he'd never experience happiness. His world was dark. In fact, it had been dark since his birth and he never seen any light in it. The Lord had never given him a break. It was just like his mother had told him; he was bad luck. It was bad luck that would haunt him until he closed his eyes for the rest of his miserable fucking life.

"I was given this life because I was the only one strong enough to live it…" He rose to his feet and lifted his head, staring at his reflection. His eyes were moist and his face was wet. He looked like a man that had gone mad and needed to be latched and strapped in a strait jacket. He'd been struggling all his life with his mental issues. The medication, the therapist, none of it helped him to cope. When his demons got the best of him, he drank long and hard. He woke up with the world's biggest migraine every time he did so. He hated alcohol. In fact, the taste of liquor made his stomach twist and turn, but alcoholic beverages were one of the few things that combatted the war inside of his head.

"I was given this life because there's some other poor bastard out there that wasn't strong enough to shoulder it. I was given this life because that man or woman would be forcing a revolver down their throat by now. I was given this life but God… oh, God…" He shut his eyelids briefly and swallowed, shaking his head. Tears flew down his cheeks, and he looked up at the ceiling. "I was given this life, but God… Goddamn it gets harder and harder to live it every day." He snorted and wiped his eyes with the inside of his shirt.

A knock at the door caught him by surprise. Quickly, he turned the dials of the faucet on and splashed water on his face before turning to the towel on the rack, patting his face dry. "Yeah, ma?" he called out over his shoulder.

"Someone named, uh, Odette is on yo' cell? You wanna talk to her?" her voice came from the opposite side of the door.

"Yeah, hold up." He took the time to dry his hands on the towel. As he was doing this, he could hear his mother telling Odette to hold on. Right after, he was unlocking and pulling the door open. The hallway was dark but, as soon as he pulled the door open, the light from inside of the bathroom illuminated her entire form.

Ella Williams was a five foot seven woman with a toffee hue. She had a big black mole by her right ear and a double chin to match with her portly body. She almost always wore her hair in a ponytail and, most of the time, you could catch her in a t-shirt and jeans, with a Newport dangling at the corner of her mouth.

His mother's forehead wrinkled seeing her son's face, as she passed him his cellular. "Kreon, have you been crying?" she asked as she gently stroked his cheek, seeing the hurt in his eyes.

"Nah, ma, I just gotta headache. You got anything for it?" he lied with a straight face.

"I may have some Excedrin P.M.; it may put chu out," she told him as her concerned eyes lingered on her son. Although he claimed he only had a headache, she had a feeling that it went deeper than that.

"It's cool, ma. You mind getting them for me, please?"

"Okay." She kissed his cheek and rubbed the side of his face, heading off to retrieve the pills he asked her for.

"Sup with it?" Kreon answered the phone like he wasn't just battling the war going on inside of his head. He plopped down on the couch and looked to the hallway. His mother stood there taking casual pulls from a Newport, watching him with a curious expression on her face. She'd grown use to his behavior, but it always puzzled her how his moods switched so often. Borderlines were different from bipolar people. See, people suffering from Borderline Personality Disorder moods changed in minutes, while people that were bipolar moods didn't change for hours or days at a time. She knew this much from doing a little research. Ella allowed her eyes to linger on her only son for a time, before walking off into the opposite direction.

"Heyyyy, how are you?" Odette's full lips stretched across her face, as she showcased that marvelous smile of hers. She rolled over from off her stomach and laid with her back on the bed, curling the cord around her finger. Her bare feet were propped upon the wall. She was dressed in a big plaid shirt that showcased her ample breasts and panties.

"I'm good, now that you reminded me of what angels sound like."

She turned red in the cheeks and smiled harder. Giggling, she smacked her hand over her lips to stop the sound. Feeling embarrassed because she was letting him know that his way with words had her smitten, she cleared her throat with a fist to her mouth. "Unh huh, I bet chu tell that to all of the girls."

"Only the beautiful ones."

She laughed and said, "Oh my God, do you have a line for everything I say?"

"These aren't lines. I'm just giving you the real."

"Is that so?"

"Facts."

Kreon and Odette went on to talk for hours that night. The time seemed to fly by because their conversation was so good. They didn't even fall asleep. Well, at least Kreon didn't. For a time, he just sat on the phone listening to

Odette lightly snoring and imagined what it was like to be in bed with her, wrapped in her arms. Once he had enough, he hung up the telephone and went to work on his manuscript. Later that day, he got a call from Odette while she was on her break at her gig. She worked at Wal-Mart. When it was time for her to come off her break, she placed the little Blu-Tooth headset on her ear and talked to him throughout the day.

On her way home from work, during her shower, her making dinner, her lying down for bed, they talked. Odette had gotten comfortable with Kreon over the next few weeks. She felt like she could be completely naked in front of him. She told him any and everything about herself, baring it all, even her deepest darkest secrets. That was one of the things that she loved about him, she could be herself without being judged. Kreon listened to her without complaint. He knew how much women liked to talk, especially about themselves. He knew this because he came from a family comprised of mostly women. Not to mention, he had dealt with a couple himself. Homie knew exactly what women desired from men. Fortunately for him, he was what they desired without even trying to be. As cliché as it may sound, the nigga was just being himself. That came effortlessly.

Although Odette let Kreon know everything about her, he wasn't so comfortable as to tell her so much about himself. When she asked, he would change the subject. Things were going well between them; she didn't want to rock the boat, so she let it slide until later. She figured when he was ready to let her in, he would. For now, she would enjoy the dream that was Kreon Williams.

Kreon and Odette had finally agreed to hang out one night. She invited him over for dinner, and he showed up with a bouquet of some of the most beautiful flowers she'd ever seen and a bottle of Apple Cider, since he couldn't drink. Upon entering her home, she introduced him to her sister, Shonda, who had dropped by to hang out that night, just so she could meet her sister's *Perfect Guy*. Although she still claimed that he was too good to be true, she couldn't help admitting that she liked homeboy. He was cool, charming, funny, and down to earth, just like her little sister claimed he was.

***

The hot shower water pelted against the back of the porcelain tub; a fog slowly began to manifest, clouding the bathroom little by little. Kreon stepped before the medicine cabinet's mirror and pulled off his shirt, tossing it aside amongst his boxer briefs and socks. He looked at himself in the mirror, taking in his five o'clock shadow and slightly nappy hair. It had been a while since he'd seen a barber, so it had started to bead and resemble an S-curl somewhat. He took note of the bags underneath his eyes and the lump on his shoulder. The doctor told him it was a skin tag and it had grown since he was 24-years-old. Now, it looked like a Milk Dud sitting up there. Next, were the stretch marks on his shoulders, arms and his hairy chest. He took in his appearance and, although he accepted it, he wasn't quite satisfied. He had once weighed 423 pounds; through dedication and hard work, he shed down to 260 pounds. He was proud of himself, but still felt like there was room for improvement.

"You had a good two weeks kicking it with old girl, huh? She cool people?"

"Yeah, I fucks with lil' momma," Kreon responded to the voice inside of his head. He didn't hear a voice, but thoughts. It was his negative thinking that always got the best of him. His mind was his greatest enemy.

"I know you do. She fucks with chu, too. But she has daddy issues, looking for her old man in every nigga that she meets."

"How you figure?" He frowned.

"Come on now, my nigga. Bitch talking 'bout she loves you within a week. Chocolate drop is looking for love. A sucka ass nigga to play hubby to her and daddy to her lil' nigga. She needs you to heal that broken heart of hers. You heard all those secrets she told you? You not 'pose to tell a nigga you tryna build something with that type of shit. Fuck she tryna do? Run you off?"

"Whatever, my nigga," He blew his frustration and his nose throbbed once. By this time, the mirror had been fogged from the steam the hot shower produced.

"I still think it was stupid of you telling her about Nigeria. Bitch didn't need to know all of that."

"Maybe not, but I keep it one hunnit. I ain't gotta lie. Either a broad gone respect it or check it. Besides, I dropped Nigeria. I'm riding with O. Shit, Nigeria made her choice when she chose to go to Tampa, instead of coming to take up time with me. Kreon don't take the backseat to nobody, mothafuck that puss ass trip! If she knew betta she'd do betta."

"See, that's what the fuck I'm talking about, that's my nigga. Stay on some playa type shit, fuck these bitchez, get money."

Kreon shook his head and opened the sliding glass door, stepping inside of the tub. He placed his hand against the tiled wall and lowered his head, allowing the hot liquid to hit his head and cascade down his form, swirling down the drain. Suddenly, his face began to twitch and he squeezed his eyelids shut, gritting. Tears came bursting through his eyes, outlining his eyelashes and eventually running down his cheeks. His shoulders and form trembled as he broke down sobbing. The sad thing about it was, he didn't even know why he was so emotional. Having his disorder, he didn't have control of his emotions… they had control of him.

Tranay Adams

CHAPTER EIGHT
The next day

Kreon made his way across the wax linoleum floor, hearing the mesh of voices of the visitors there to see their loved ones. His head was on swivel, looking around for the man that he had come to see himself. It had been quite some time since he had seen, Drennen, but he knew now was as good a time as any, being that he didn't really have much to do that day.

Kreon had known Drennen for as long as he could remember. The young man looked at him and Omar as his surrogate fathers. He got both advice and life lessons from them. Although Drennen had been locked up, they kept in contact through the older man's contraband cellphone. Kreon also made it his business to drop at least $100 on his books a month, for him to get whatever he needed inside. He knew that what he was giving him wasn't much, seeing as how the commissary in the pen was expensive but reasoned that something was better than nothing. It wasn't like homie needed it though. Omar made sure that there was always money on his books, so he could eat. Kreon didn't care though. He reasoned that his uncle's money was his own and he had to give his own contribution to his big homie.

Seeing a vacant stool ahead and Drennen approaching, Kreon made his way over. Upon sitting down, he picked up the telephone and waited for the man of the hour to sit before him. The five-foot-seven Drennen sat down on the stool, wearing a crisp, clean uniform. He wore gold frames on his face and a small crucifix around his neck. His low-cut temple fade swirled with 360° waves. He had a small button nose and thin, dark lips that led anyone that had met him to believe he smoked weed. Homie possessed a medium build and tattoos that hid the secret of his past.

Although he was smiling, the teardrops inked at the corner of his right-eye let niggaz know that he was with the shit.

"Sup with it, youngsta?" he greeted his street son with a big ass smile that stretched across his face. Surprisingly, the jovial expression made him look approachable.

"Ain't shit, family, holdin' on like a hubcap in the fast lane." Kreon cracked a grin. "Look at chu though, OG, you getting big as a mothafucka up in here."

"Yeah, a nigga been doing a lil' something, something behind the wall." He lifted his arm and clenched his fists, showcasing his small muscle gains he'd gotten while on lock. "Ain't shit to do up in this mothafucka besides read and try to work out. Shit, if I'm not doing that, then a nigga jerking off or knocking out some of these ol' busta ass niggaz up in here." He stopped to mad-dog one of the inmates that had just came through the visitation room door.

Kreon looked back and forth between his street daddy and the nigga he was grilling. He couldn't help but wonder what was up between the two of them. "Sup, Drennen?"

"Yo, Scar!" Drennen called out to the inmate. He was a tall, dark caramel cat. His hair was permed and he wore it in two small pigtails on either side of his head. A nasty scar aligned his jaw. When Drennen called out to him, he turned around with a hard face that would have caused less of a man to shit himself.

"Watts up wit it, Blood?" He threw his head back.

"You owe me, youngsta. A nigga need that, ASAP." A line creased his forehead because he couldn't believe this nigga was acting like he didn't know what the deal was.

"On some real shit, I'm fucked up in here. You gon' have to charge that shit to the game."

"Charge it to the game?" Drennen's brows furrowed. He chuckled to hide how pissed off he was. The nigga's blood was boiling hot with rage.

"Fuck is you, hard of hearing or something? Pardon my back," he said as he turned his back to him and went on about his business, walking down the aisle like a straight up G. He had a demeanor that told everyone around him that he was *untouchable.*

Drennen turned back around to Kreon, smiling even harder. His eyes were glassy too. That nigga Kreon had seen this look before, so he already knew what time it was. Homie that had just disrespected his big homie was going to pay dearly for it, and Drennen was going to see to it.

"You good?" Kreon asked, concerned.

"I'm straight, youngin'. You know how I do." He looked him dead in his eyes. Without saying a word, he communicated to his little homie that he was going to break Scar's ass off something real proper like. "Anyway, fuck that bitch ass nigga, how you been?"

Drennen switched the subject and they chopped it up for a minute. Before long, the correctional officer guarding the door that the inmates came through was telling him that it was time to go.

"Before I raise up, you know I'm 'bouta be up outta here in a minute, right?" Drennen asked, already knowing that Kreon knew he was coming home shortly. Still, he nodded yes. "I heard about that situation that you and ya' moms are having at y'all lil' apartment over there. If you want, as soon as I touch down, I could..." he nodded his head, letting him know that he would put Tranisha's punk ass to sleep for him. All he had to do was give him the okay and it was done.

"Thanks, Drennen, but I'll handle it."

"You sho'? You know that's my M.O.," he said lowly, as he looked around to make sure no one was looking at him; then, on the low, he made his hand into the shape of a gun at his side.

"I'm good," he said, cracking a grin.

"Alright then, loved one, I'm gone." He rose from his stool and made his way towards the door where the correctional officer was. His eyes came across a scowling Scar; he smiled, thinking about his impending doom.

"Ol' mark ass nigga." Scar shook his head, pitifully.

***

Kreon nodded his head, as he coasted through the streets with one hand gripping the steering wheel. His shoulder was slumped to the left and he was massaging his chin as he gangsta leaned. Tyrese's *'Baby Boy'* was pumping from the speakers, rattling the door panels. Coming to a stop at a red light, he looked to his right and saw a very familiar man in a priest uniform. He was greeting the people that were coming through the door of his holy domain. He was an almond complexioned cat with a shaved head. He had salt and pepper facial stubble that formed his goatee. He had on glasses and a simple Timex watch. He greeted him, following with handshakes and pleasant smiles. This made Kreon scowl and twist his lips. He knew this mothafucka like the back of his hand, and he sure as hell wasn't a man of the cloth. Nah, this cock sucka was as wicked as they came.

Flashback

"Get... get cho ass up in there!" Khadafi hollered, shoving young Kreon inside of the closet. The boy tried his damndest to get out, but his father's kicking and pushing him back kept him at a standstill. Kreon had fallen back inside of the closet. When he stuck his arm out of the cracked, opened door, Khadafi slammed the door on it and he hollered out in agony. His arm slithered back inside, but not before the door was slammed on it again. Breathing heavy and with a scowling face, Khadafi slammed the closet door shut. He then stuck a folding chair underneath

the door knob so that his son couldn't get out. Afterwards, he picked up his Old English can of beer and took it to the head, throat moving up and down his neck as he guzzled. He took one last look at the closet and licked his lips, before heading out of the bedroom.

Inside of the closet, Kreon rubbed the lump that had begun to form on his arm. Sniffing and whimpering, tears flooding down his cheeks. Wiping his face with the back of his fist, he scrambled over to the door and twisted the lock back and forth. The door was locked. This sent him in a panic. His heart was beating like an African drum inside of his chest.

"Pleeeease, lemme out! Lemme outta here!" Young Kreon pounded against the closet door with his fist, as tears burst and cascaded down his cheeks. He was locked inside of the closet, and the only light was the yellow one that shined from beneath the door. "Dad, please, I can't breathe in here!" The small space was full of clothes and sneakers. There was barely space for him to move and air was scarce. "Haa! Haa! Haa! Haa! Haa! Haa! Haa! Haa! Haa!" He threw his head back and hyperventilated, struggling to take oxygen into his lungs. It was hot inside of the closet and his entire body was feeling warm. He was terrified now. He had asthma and was starting to feel faint, due to lack of fresh air.

Realizing this, Kreon placed his mouth to the opening underneath the door and sucked in as much air as he could. The air that he could get into his lung calmed him down a little, but he was still crying. His whimpers grew smaller and smaller until they disappeared, and he settled down. Finding himself growing sleepy, he got into a fetal position and drifted off to sleep. He dreamt of a place where none of his worries existed and all his favorites were present.

Present

Kreon was in a trance, staring at Khadafi through hateful eyes with lips twisted up. He had it in mind to grab his .38 from underneath the seat, hop up out of his whip, and give it to that nigga in broad daylight. He didn't know it, but his nostril and his top lip twitched. He was so engrossed in his thoughts, he didn't hear the cars behind him honking their horns at him until one of them had hopped out of their vehicle. It was a short white man with sandy brown hair and eyeglasses a little too big for his face. Obviously pissed the fuck off, he stopped at the driver side window and leaned forth, knocking on the glass. Once Kreon didn't answer, he adjusted his glasses and knocked at the window again. Kreon blinked his eyelids repeatedly and looked around to the driver side window, letting the window down.

"Sup with it?"

"I've gotta go to work, pal. Do you mind moving it along?"

Kreon nodded and smashed off, leaving the white dude heading back to his ride. He looked up in his rearview mirror; Khadafi was growing smaller and smaller as he drove away. This happened until he had disappeared before his eyes. Before Kreon knew it, he was pulling up at Odette's house and hopping out.

That night

Cling! Clink! Dinggg!

Scar yanked back and forth on the pipe that he was handcuffed to. Once he figured out that the chain attached to the metal bracelet wasn't going to break, he stopped his struggling and scanned his surroundings. That's when he realized he was inside of the boiler room. It was dark, wet, and light was scarce. He heard the occasional droplets of brown water splashing into a small puddle on the surface.

Afterwards, he looked to his right and saw a couple of big, fat ass rats traveling along a large rusty pipe.

"What that shit do, my nigga?" a voice resonated throughout the boiler room. A light shined at Scar's back and he turned around. The C.O. that came to get him from out of his cell and cuffed him to the pipe was standing at his rear, holding a flashlight to him. Beside him was a short man patting a steel pipe in his palm, heading in his direction. He was the nigga that had called at his back.

Scar threw his freehand above his brows and narrowed his eyelids, trying to see who was coming in his direction. The closer the man patting the pipe in his palm came, the more of him that filled out until he was completely visible. Scar's eyes bulged as he gasped. He went back to trying to yank loose from the pipe that he was handcuffed to, but his efforts were futile. There just wasn't any use. Heart beating fast, chest jumping up and down, his head snapped around to the man that had come to pay him a visit. It was Drennen.

Drennen smiled, looking sinister like he was back in the visitation room when Kreon came to see him. Letting the pipe hang at his side, he reached inside of his pocket and pulled out a crisp, folded one-hundred-dollar bill. Turning to the C.O., he slid the dead president into his uniform's pocket and patted it gently. Next, he removed his glasses and passed them to him. Calm and steady, he made his way towards Scar, who had started back pulling and yanking on the handcuff that was attached to the pipe. The closer Drennen drew in, the more his shadow eclipsed the flashlight's ray that was illuminating his intended victim.

Right when he was on top of his enemy, he whipped around. It was then that he felt the first blow from the pipe, which collided with the side of his face. There was a sickening crack sound that let him know that he'd broken his jaw as he crashed to the ground. Scar's mouth moved like a fish out of water as he grabbed at Drennen's pants leg. A scowling Drennen snatched his leg back and kicked him square in the mouth, sending blood specks flying and dotting the surface. Afterwards, he went to work on him, slamming the pipe into every place on his body that was left exposed. The beating was so brutal that the correctional officer cringed and looked away. Drennen didn't give a fuck, though. Nah, he kept at it until his weapon was stained crimson and he was breathing heavily. His face was coated in perspiration and his brow dripped wetness. He took the time to wipe his forehead with the back of his hand before kicking his victim across the chin, knocking him out cold.

With the deed done, Drennen slipped his glasses back on and whipped out a rag from his back pocket. Once he'd finished wiping the pipe clean, he used it to pass the C.O. the pipe. He then patted him on his shoulder and went on about his business, leaving him alone with Scar. The C.O. unlocked Scar from the handcuff and left him where he was, battered, bruised and snoring awkwardly.

The only sound was Drennen whistling as he strolled down the corridor, shadow casted on the right wall as he went along.

***

Knock! Knock! Knock!

The rapping at the door startled Odette, as she shot to her feet. She pulled off the oven mittens and darted into the bathroom where she looked the medicine cabinet mirror, fixing her hair the best she could. Afterwards, she ran out of the bathroom into the living room, where Marquise was sitting Indian-style playing his Game Boy. She pulled him up to his feet and took the Game Boy out of his hand, sitting it aside on the coffee table. She went about the task of straightening out the wrinkles in his clothing, adjusting the collar of his shirt. Once she was done, she brushed the lint off his head with her hand and cupped his cute little face, kissing his cheeks affectionately.

"Okay. You ready to meet mommy's new boyfriend?"

"Yes." He smiled, showcasing his dimples and big gap between his top row of teeth.

"Okay." She smiled at her little man and interlocked her fingers with his, approaching the front door. After taking a deep breath, she undid the locks of the door and pulled it open. On the opposite side, she found Kreon holding a bouquet of roses. He wore a one-sided smile and a black, Ralph Lauren sweat suit with the red logo. On his feet was a pair of all-white Air Force Ones.

"Are those for me?" Odette looked from the roses to Kreon, smiling.

"Yeah, these are for you." He passed them to her and sweetly kissed her on the cheek.

"Thank you." She blushed and smiled harder. A man had never given her flowers before, so she was flattered to have been given some by him. "Come in." She stepped aside and allowed him inside. He crossed the threshold, and she shut the door behind him. "Lemme put these in water and check on this chicken. I'll be right back."

Once Odette had left, Kreon turned to her son while smirking. "What's up, lil' nigga? What's yo' name?"

"My name is Marquise, but my mom and my T.T. call me, Mar Mar," he stated proudly. "What's your name?"

Kreon pulled his sweats up and kneeled to him, wearing a jovial expression. "I'm Kreon, Mar Mar."

"Nice to meet chu." The little fella outstretched his hand for a handshake.

"Nah, nah, nah, that's too formal. If we're gonna be homies, then we've gotta come up with our own handshakes. How about that?"

"Okay." Marquise jumped up and down excitedly.

Kreon practiced a complex handshake with Marquise about three times before he finally learned it.

"Alright, my main man." He and the little boy chuckled.

"You wanna play the game with me?"

"Smooth."

Marquise grabbed him by the hand and led him over to the couch. He sat where he was perched, watching the little nigga set up his game system and occasionally glancing at his smiling mother. She was standing in the kitchen doorway, watching how fast her son had taken to the new man in her life.

"Alright, you ready?" Marquise passed his guest one controller and he kept the other.

"I stay ready, family."

"I'm finna kick yo' butt in Street Fighter, watch." He smiled amusingly.

"We'll see." He leaned forward, balancing the controller in his hands while his eyes focused on the flat-screen tv. Marquise was positioned the same way that he was, eyes glued to the tube. Odette watched them for a little while, before going back inside of the kitchen to finish cooking. The fellas laughed and joked, playing the PS4. Afterwards, they ate dinner and watched *PJ Mask* until Marquise fell asleep. The little dude was lying across Kreon's lap, snoring like a piglet.

"Look at him." A smiling Odette nudged Kreon and nodded to her slumbering son. He looked down at him and smiled, caressing the side of his curly haired head affectionately. "He looks so angelic lying there in your lap. He really likes you, you know?"

"I really like him too. He's a good kid." He continued to caress the side of his head.

"Come on, I'm going to lay him down in bed." She grabbed Marquise by one of his arms to pick him up. That's when he started talking with his eyelids shut.

"No, mommy. I want Kreon to tuck me in."

Odette looked to Kreon for his approval; he nodded yes. With that out of the way, he picked him up into his arms and carried him off to bed. After throwing the blanket aside, he laid the little dude down and covered him up. Marquise, with his eyes still shut, turned over in bed where he was lying. Kreon rubbed the side of his head and then kissed it. Heading for the bedroom door, he heard him call for him behind his back, prompting him to turn around.

"I love you," the little dude said genuinely.

Kreon stared at him, smiling for a second before responding, "I love you too, lil' man."

With that said, he left the door, pulling it shut behind him and journeying down the hallway. Returning to the living room, he found Odette with her back against the arm of the couch, sipping what looked like red wine. The flat-screen displayed burning logs, which she was staring at pleasantly. Her iPod was on its doc and Aaliyah's *At Your Best* was serenading the scene as she nodded her head to the music, slightly snapping her fingers. Her hair was pulled back in a bun and she was in silk pajamas; her pretty toes showed off her French manicured toes. She was in her own world at the moment, unaware that Kreon had returned. He stood at the entrance of the living room inside of the hallway, watching her with an intrigued expression across his face. It amazed him how she'd set everything up so fast. He couldn't help thinking that she had the speed of The Flash or some shit.

"You work fast, Mocha." He started in her direction, smiling.

This caused her eyelids to peel open; she looked to him, smiling. "Nahhh, just a lil' something, something ya' girl threw together." Kreon looked at everything again, nodding his approval. "Would you like some wine?" She held up the expensive black bottle of alcohol that she only popped open on special occasions.

"Nah, I'm straight. I don't really fuck with Al like that." He plopped down on the couch. She leaned over to sit the bottle down on the coffee table and sat back against the arm of the sofa. He sat her feet in his lap and began massaging them. This caused a soft moan to escape her lips and she shut her eyelids briefly, enjoying the moment. A nigga had never touched her feet before. His touch was so inviting. In fact, him touching her feet caused her pussy to jump, but she wasn't about to give him some yet. Nah, she wasn't about to come off like some hoe, no matter how much she was feeling him.

"You like that?" he asked, looking at her.

"Unh huh." She nodded with her eyelids still shut, taking a sip from her wine glass. "Mmmm, your hands are magical."

"Well, wait 'til you get some of this diiiiiiiiiick." He made a funny face that caused her to bust out laughing, playfully slapping his arm.

The laughter settled down between them and she continued to partake in her wine.

"Yo' ass is so goofy, bae. Why are you so goofy?"

"I don't know." He shrugged. "A nigga just tryna make it through the darkness, ya griff me?"

"Let's talk about that."

"About what?"

"The darkness."

Kreon took on a serious expression and said, "Listen, I don't ever want to talk about what I've been through... ever, under any circumstances. If you can deal with that, then you and I can keep this thing of ours going, but if not, well… I'm sure you can use your imagination." He looked her in the eyes and awaited her decision.

She took a deep breath and said, "Okay, alright."

"Are you sure?" He looked at her with an eyebrow raised.

"Yes." She nodded and smiled, sitting her glass of wine down on the coffee table. "Now, let's cuddle."

Kreon kicked his Chucks off and pulled off his other shirt, leaving himself in his undershirt. He laid back on the couch and motioned her over; she laid against him and looked at peace in his arms. She shut her eyelids and laid her delicate hand against his chest. He combed his fingers through her individual braids and kissed the top of her head tenderly. Shutting his eyelids, he laid his head back against the arm of the couch. Their chest rose and fell slowly, falling asleep shortly thereafter.

Tranay Adams

CHAPTER NINE
One week later

Kreon found himself kicking it with his uncle for most of the day, checking his traps and handling other business. They had just left from eating dinner at Hometown Buffet, chopping it up over their meals and shit. Kreon loved the place; he remembered his uncle used to take him and his cousin, Jaekwon, there frequently. In fact, he stayed taking the family out to amusement parks, movie theaters, and other places of entertainment. This was way back in the 90's, when crack money was sweet and snitching wasn't at an all-time high like it was in the 2000's. Old Omar was doing all right for himself. He wasn't doing that bad now, but he wasn't doing as nearly as good as he was back then. But still, he wasn't hurting for nothing.

Like always, Kreon picked his uncle's brain about every aspect of the game. Now, some of the aspects he didn't need to hear because he was what you would consider small time but, then again, he never knew when he may want to take things to another level. As far as his future went, he didn't see himself working a square gig like he did when he was working at the school board. Nah, he wanted money, lots and lots of money. And he didn't see himself making as much as he wanted slaving at a nine to five.

"So, what was the pen like?"

"What chu mean?" Omar looked both ways before making a left turn.

"I mean, is it anything like the movies? Do niggaz actually be gettin' stabbed up and raped like that up in there? Or is it all just some fabricated bullshit?"

"Shit, man, I done seen tall, skinny niggaz like that nigga, Jaekwon, size get talked outta they ass," he said seriously, stopping at a red stop light. "Can you believe it?

Nigga gettin' talked outta his manhood? Fools didn't put up a fight or nothing, willin' to just let a nigga run up in his shit-hole." He shook his head, pitifully. "Man, prison don't bring shit outta you that ain't already in you, Kre. If you a G out in these streets but a pussy deep down inside, then them cement walls gone bring it outta you, bruh, straight up." The sunlight deflected off his Rolex chain and his matching watch, casting two, small colorful rainbows.

"True that," Kreon conceded, focusing his attention out of the passenger side window. Ever since Kreon was 11-years-old, his uncle had been giving him gems. A lot of times, his uncle thought that he wasn't listening, but then he heard how he conducted himself out in the streets and saw how he moved for himself. It was because of this, he knew his nephew had held on to his words like they were scriptures straight out of the Holy Bible.

Omar parked his whip beneath the underground parking complex of his building. He and Kreon jumped out, slamming their doors shut and making their way towards the chocolate brown door that housed the elevators. They boarded the elevators, chopping it up like they were back inside of his ride. Once the elevator doors opened, they stepped out and rounded the corridor, heading towards the unit that Omar and Candy lived in. Before Kreon knew it, they were entering his uncle's apartment and he was shutting the door behind him, locking it.

"The usual, right?" Omar pointed at him, as he trekked down the hallway towards his bedroom.

"And you know this, man," Kreon said, mimicking Smokey from the movie *Friday*, a smirk forming across his face. His uncle ducked off to get the drugs he planned on purchasing and he found himself alone, staring ahead at nothing. Plain face, eyes still, he zoned out and found himself at another place and time.

Khadafi wasn't the easiest person to live with, being that he'd get drunk and berate people, namely Kreon. He ridiculed the young man about his size and the way that his clothes fit him, constantly driving his self-esteem to the ground. Often, the youth fell asleep while crying his eyes out, cursing himself for ever being born. One day, while his mother was pulling a 16-hour shift at her job as a caregiver, Kreon was getting a verbal lashing from his old man about how he needed to lose some weight before his fat ass had a heart attack at 11-years-old. Kreon told him to go fuck himself and slammed the bathroom door shut. He'd just stripped down and climbed inside of the tub, when the door came bursting open. A furious Khadafi rushed inside and tried to drown him for his blatant disrespect, but he managed to knee his ass in the balls. The miserable mothafucka fell to his knees, holding his privates and Kreon dashed out of the bathroom, running as fast as he could.

"You lil' fat fucka, I'ma beat the black offa yo' ass!" *Khadafi called out from the other room.*

"Haa! Haa! Haa! Haa," A butt naked Kreon came running across the hardwood floor of the living room while occasionally glancing over his shoulder, eyes wide as saucers. He was wet and dripping water everywhere, leaving his wet foot imprints in his wake. He suddenly slipped and fell, falling hard on the side of his face, wincing.

Hearing his father's hurried footsteps coming in his direction, young Kreon shook off his daze and slowly tried to get to his feet. He was too late though, because Khadafi's Kufi-wearing ass was already on him. He kicked the youth in his rear and sent his head slamming back down into the hardwood surface. He then yanked his worn, thick leather belt free from the loops in his corduroy pants and went to work, beating his son like he'd ran off his plantation. He swung the belt wide and wildly. It whistled through the air and licked at his back furiously. Swack! Swack! Swack! Crack! Whack! Redness and welts formed on Kreon's back, arms, and legs as he tried to shield himself from the onslaught of lashes. He balled up like a fetus, screaming louder and louder.

"Aaaahhhhhh! Aahhhhhh! Ahhh! Ahhhhh!"

Kreon's very own screams caused his eardrums to ring, giving them an eerie feeling. He could literally feel every lash that landed against his hide. The belt came fast, furious, and without mercy, landing on every exposed part of him. The remorseless switch stung and bruised his flesh, causing welts to form all over him. He felt like he had been drenched in gasoline and set on fire. That's how hot he was from being brutally assaulted by the tyrant standing over him, his hand moving up, down, and across. The drunken bastard was trying to beat him to death.

A wincing Kreon smacked his hands over his ears and tilted his head down. Eyelids squeezed shut, he screamed at the top of his lungs. He twisted from side to side, continuing his screaming.

"Aarrrh! Grrraaahhhh! Rahhhhh!"

"Kreon! Kreeoon! Kreeeooon!" Omar called out to his nephew. Brown paper bag in one hand, he shook him as best as he could, raining spittle in his face. "Kreeeeooon!" He hollered out in his face, a thick vein swelled at his neck and another one bulged at his temple. The young nigga'z head bobbled back and forth fast, nearly touching his chest from being shaken so hard. Finally, his eyelids snapped open; he looked around as if he was seeing through his eyes for the first time. His uncle stared him in the face while breathing heavily, chest pumping madly. He swallowed the spit in his throat and a line went across his forehead, as he probed his nephew's eyes for what was going on with him. "Are... are you okay?"

Kreon looked at his arms and hands, seeing the welts that Khadafi had given him long ago. He felt on his arms and could feel them, his bruises, wincing as he did so. He squeezed his eyelids shut, then peeled them back open. The welts and bruises had vanished like they were never there. His head snapped up and he locked eyes with Omar again, breathing like he was doing now.

"I'm... I'm fucked up, Unc. I'm so fucked up." Kreon's eyes misted with tears and he snorted. He licked his lips, wiping his eyes with the back of his fist. "That nigga ruined my life. He stole my childhood. What I have become, the way I look at things... I owe a great deal of it to him."

"Fucked up how, Kre? What chu mean?" Concern spread across his face.

Kreon bit down on his bottom lip and shook his head, tears jetting down his cheeks. He turned away, not wanting his uncle to see him so vulnerable. Approaching the wall, he placed his hand against it and began pounding his forehead against it.

"These fuckin' demons, man! These fuckin' demons are clawin' at my back. It's like I can't get away from them," he sobbed, his cheeks flooding with moisture.

Seeing his nephew's reckless behavior, Omar took him by the shoulder and turned him to face him. He was shuddering and crying. His red webbed eyes dripping teardrops as he gritted.

"What's... what's wrong? What's happened to you?" He gripped his shoulder affectionately.

"You don't wanna know, man. It's so much shit, it's so much shit inside of here." He pounded his fists against his temples, rattling his head, causing teardrops to fall fast. His uncle grabbed his wrist and pulled them down from his nephew's head, letting them fall to his sides.

"Look at me, man! Look me in my eyes!" he ordered him, gripping the back of his neck until he was sure that he had his attention. "Talk to me now, tell me about these demons that occupy yo' head."

By the time Kreon had finished telling his uncle all the shit that Khadafi had done to him, tears were sliding down his face. The O.G. sniffled and wiped his eyes with the side of his fists. He bit down on his bottom lip; he motioned his nephew over. Hesitantly, Kreon rose to his feet and approached his uncle. They gave one another a manly embrace and more tears fell from the rims of his uncle's eyes. His eyes were moist and pink, looking like glass.

"I'm sorry, Kre. I'm so fuckin' sorry, man."

"Unc, it's alright, you didn't know."

Omar held his nephew at arm's length and said, "Well, now, I do and this mothafucka gon' pay for his sins. He'll be the Lord's to deal with once I'm done with him." He swore, with eyes that bled seriousness.

If that nigga Omar claimed he was going to do something, then you best believe that it was as good as done.

The next morning

Candy pulled up in front of the mega church and murdered the engine of Omar's Excursion. Her eyes were hidden behind oversized designer shades and she was chewing on bubble gum, blowing huge pink bubbles until they burst. Leaning forward, she kissed Omar deep and hard, hearing the saliva slosh around inside of their mouths. She pulled away, wiping the extra spit from the corners of her mouth. Omar's lips stretched across his five o'clock shadowed face, as he chewed on the gum that was just inside of his side chick's mouth. He kissed her one more time on the lips, before grabbing his burner out of the glove-box and tucking it on his hip.

Throwing open the driver side door, he jumped down into the street and slammed the door shut behind him.

Adjusting the collar of his red Dickie button-down, he looked at his surroundings before going on about his business. The moment his red, All-Star Chuck Taylor's touched the curb, he could hear the loud music playing on the organs of the piano. He also heard the choir singing along with the glorious tune that was being played. There wasn't any doubt in Omar's mind that Khadafi was the man behind that piano. Knowing this, he shook his head pitifully. The priest was as crooked as a barrel of snakes and he was surely going to burn in hell doing such evil in the Lord's house.

Omar was about halfway to the steps of the church before he narrowed his eyelids from the blinding rays of the sun. He pulled his sunglasses from out of his shirt's pocket and slid them onto his face. Still in motion, he kept his stride heading for the entrance of the place of worship. Coming up the steps, he heard the organs stop playing. As soon as he crossed the threshold into the building, he saw the priest talking to the choir as they gathered their things to leave. Once they had gotten everything together, the priest was seeing them off to the front door. Looking up, he saw Omar and broke out instantly in a sweat. See, this fucking slime ball used to buy his drugs off him and he was afraid of having his shady past revealed before his sheep.

As soon as his followers were gone, Khadafi turned his attention to the OG.

"Omar, good to see you; what brings you here?" He debuted a fake ass smile, showcasing the gold crown inside of his grill.

"I gotta business proposition for you, big dawg." He threw his chunky arm around the nigga'z neck and walked him down the aisle, giving him the rundown that he had in mind. "I figure you can get the shit out there, since you a man of the cloth and all. The Boys ain't gone expect a man of God to be transporting them birds, you feel me?"

"Sounds good, really good," Khadafi replied. He was comfortable now, massaging his chin as he thought about the business proposition that had been presented to him.

"You ain't on that shit no mo', are you?" He raised an eyebrow.

"Nah, nah, nah, I've been clean now for years." He stood upright, adjusting the collar of his blazer. Now, he and Omar were standing in the aisle. The domain of the Lord was dimly lit, but the sunlight shining through the entrance illuminated them.

"My man." Omar took the time to adjust Khadafi's blazer collar and smoothed it out. "Okay. I want you to be at my place at seven o'clock tonight. Cool?" The nigga nodded yes and he patted him on his shoulder. "Good." He pulled out a small cellphone and told him that his number was stored in it, slipping it inside of his shirt's pocket. Patting him on the cheek, Omar walked off whistling Dixie.

That night

"So, is homie coming over here tonight?" Jaekwon asked from where he was leaned back against the kitchen counter. He and Omar were passing a smoldering blunt between them, smoke lingering in the air.

"Yeah." Omar took the blunt from his nephew, dumping its ashes into an ashtray. "Matta fact, he shoulda been here a few minutes ago."

The doorbell chimed and Omar looked alive, passing the blunt back to his nephew. "That's him," He cleared his throat with his fist to his mouth and headed to the front door. After he unlocked and unchained the door, he pulled it open and stepped aside so that Khadafi could enter. As soon as he crossed the threshold, he shut the door behind him and led him inside of the kitchen, chopping it up along the way. "You late."

"I know, sorry about that," he apologized, adjusting the collar of his overcoat. "It's hella traffic out there."

"Sure, sure, sure, have a seat." Omar motioned to the chair at the kitchen table. As soon as he did, the crooked ass priest sat down. "Can I offer you somethin' to eat or drink, Khadafi?" Omar inquired, rummaging through the refrigerator.

"Nah, I'm okay." He waved him off. Seeing Jaekwon at the counter, he decided to speak. "How're you doin', Jaekwon? How's ya motha?"

Jaekwon stood there, eye balling him while getting high. He didn't reply to him at all. As far as he was concerned, that nigga could suck a big bag of dicks. The expression on the young thug's face made Khadafi uneasy, but he decided to pay him no mind. He was there on business and, as soon as it was conducted, he was out of there.

"You sho'? I could have Jaekwon hook you up with a sandwich," Omar offered, taking sips from a can of Coca Cola.

Khadafi's stomach growled, hearing the O.G. mention a sandwich. Truthfully, the story he had given them about being late because of traffic was bullshit. He was actually at one of his follower's home, banging his wife's back out, which he did every night once the clueless bastard went to work at nine o'clock. Anyway, he'd told his fuck-buddy to make him something to eat but, once he saw her fine naked ass come out of the shower dripping wet, he changed his mind and dove straight into the pussy. Now, here he was, hungry as a mothafucking hostage. He wanted that sandwich that Omar offered bad as shit, but he sure as hell wasn't about to take it. He didn't want that nigga Jaekwon making him a goddamn thing that he planned on eating. There wasn't any telling what he may do to it when his back was turned.

"Nah, I'm alright. Like I told Jaekwon here, I'm ready to get down to business." He drummed his fingertips on the table top impatiently.

"Alright," Omar sat his Coca Cola down on the table, "lemme go get the merchandise." He headed out of the kitchen to get the kilos that homeboy would be transporting. While he was gone, Khadafi and Jaekwon locked eyes for a time, no one blinking. Suddenly, the young thug glanced to the right, seeing someone. The crooked ass priest's eyelids narrowed. When he saw a shadow approaching him from behind on the table top, he went to turn around, but it was already too late.

"Yuuuck!" Khadafi's eyes bulged and watered. His lips quivered and his tongue hung out the side of his mouth. The chair he was sitting in tilted back on the hind legs. He struggled while trying to get loose, pulling on the fishing line. Kreon's brows furrowed and he gritted his teeth. His face shined from perspiration, droplets falling to the floor. His gloved hands tightened their grasps around the fishing line as he pulled back further. His weight brought Khadafi and the chair to the surface, falling on him. "Gaaaah!" The priest's legs kicked wildly and his black leather shoes left scuff marks on the linoleum.

"Bitch ass nigga, you thought chu was gone keep yo' life after all that foul ass shit you did to me? Huh? Grrrrrrr!" Kreon threw his head back and pulled back further, the line tightening around his gloved hands. Sweat stains had formed underneath the arms of his t-shirt and collar. That son of a bitch Khadafi wasn't going out that easy; he was putting up one hell of a fight.

Omar had just stepped through the doorway of the kitchen, Desert Eagle with a silencer on its barrel at his side. With sloped eyebrows and a wrinkled forehead, he witnessed his nephew commit murder for the first time. Quickly, he glanced at Jaekwon, seeing him watching too.

Khadafi's movements began to grow slower and slower, the more pressure Kreon applied.

"Die! Die, goddamn it! Die!" Kreon jerked on the line violently, and something snapped. The priest's head fell to the right, hanging in a grotesque manner. His eyes were wide, staring out into space, and tongue stuck out the side of his mouth. He was dead. The victim released his bowels one last time and he threw his head aside, face tightening while having gotten a whiff of the repugnant stench.

Omar's face balled up and he turned his head, getting a whiff of a foul stench in the air.

"Goddamn, Blood, stink!" A disgusted Jaekwon smacked his hand over his nose and mouth, causing his gold chain to rock from left to right. His face frowned up; Khadafi's dead, funky ass had the entire mothafucking kitchen lit. Jaekwon's cheeks inflated and deflated; he was trying not to vomit all over the floor. The stench was really fucking with his stomach.

Kreon unwrapped the fishing line from around Khadafi's carcass and got up from off the floor. He sat the fishing line on the kitchen table and staggered over to the cupboard, taking down a glass. He turned on the faucet and filled the glass with water, huffing and puffing. Afterwards, he wiped his beaded forehead with the back of his hand. He turned the glass up and drunk it down, his throat rolling up and down. Taking the glass from his lips, he looked back at Khadafi. Scowling, he marched over to him and kicked the hell out of him. The carcass shook, but the spirit that had inhabited was long gone. That didn't stop Kreon from kicking him in the face repeatedly though. He didn't stop until his lifeless victim's face looked like bloody hamburger meat. After this, he was breathing hard and mad-dogging the corpse, spitting on the body.

When Kreon turned around to Omar and Jaekwon, they saw tears sliding down his face rapidly. His eyes were pink and glassy, having gotten his revenge after all these years were sweet. Sex hadn't given him nearly as much pleasure as he'd gotten from strangling Khadafi to death. That sensation had come and gone though, and was now replaced with great emotion pain and heartache. Although that bastard Khadafi was gone, the mental scars that he left behind with Kreon would last his lifetime. Thinking of that was enough to make the young man cry.

"Come here. man." Omar threw his arm around Kreon's neck and pulled him into a manly hug, allowing him to cry his eyes out against his chest. The O.G. could feel the wetness of his tears, seeking through the fabric of his shirt and the vibration of him against his chest as he wailed. "It's okay, nephew, it's okay now. He's gone and he can't hurt chu now." He kissed him on top of the head and looked to Jaekwon, motioning him over with a wave of his gun. Jaekwon, who was still staring at Khadafi's dead body, gathered himself mentally and rose from off the kitchen sink. He joined his cousin and uncle in a group hug, rubbing his hand up and down Kreon's back to comfort him.

Kreon broke his embrace, wiping his eyes with his t-shirt and sniffling. His eyes were still glassy and pink but, now, his nose was red from sniffling and crying. He looked from his relatives to the dead body he created. The thought of that bitch ass nigga, Khadafi, resting in peace caused him to instantly scowl. He was glad that black-hearted son of a bitch was dead.

"Alright, it's time," Omar told Jaekwon, causing him to frown up. He didn't know what the fuck he was talking about.

"What chu mean, Unc?" Jaekwon inquired, brows crinkled.

"We're all in this together. If one goes down, then we all go down. You know how I do." Omar turned to

Khadafi's body and pointed the banger at him. Pulling the trigger, the corpse jerked violent upon impact of the copper slug. After the first shot, he squeezed off one more and then tried to pass it to Jaekwon. He wouldn't accept it.

"Nah, I'm good." Jaekwon held up his hands, palm showing. It was clear that he didn't want anything to do with the ritual his uncle had in mind.

"Fuck you mean, *'Nah, I'm good'*?" Omar's face balled up. "You know the rules, homeboy."

"Ain't no need of me poppin' this fool, he dead," he reasoned, kicking Khadafi's corpse. His sudden movement caused his chain to swing back and forth.

"You know what? Fuck it. I ain't got time to argue witchu," Omar said, passing the gun to Kreon. The young man stepped to the body of the deceased, pointing the deadly end of his weapon down at him. His eyebrows dipped and lines formed across his nose, as he pulled the trigger twice. The impact from the bullets caused Khadafi's form to jerk violently. Once the gun finished bucking, the last of the shell casings danced as they fell to the floor. He held the Desert Eagle in the same position he had when he opened fire, smoke wafting from its barrel. Omar took the gun from him with a red bandana and folded it up in it, tucking it into the small of his back.

"Alright, y'all help me carry this nigga into the front, so we can roll 'em up in the rug and dump 'em," Omar commanded of his nephews, and they obliged him. "You sure you okay with participating in this, Mr. Jaekwon?" He frowned, not feeling how his nephew was acting at the moment.

"I'm good. Now, let's get this shit ova with." Jaekwon walked to the middle of the floor, prepared to help his cousin and uncle with disposing of the dead body.

"Alright then, come on," Omar said, kneeling to the body alongside his nephews.

Unbeknownst to Kreon and Omar, their murdering of Khadafi had been recorded by small surveillance cameras that were the rubies in the gold tiger's head medallion.

***

Kreon came through the door flanked by Omar and Jaekwon. He shut the door behind them and tossed his keys onto the coffee table. Afterwards, he walked to his mother's bedroom and opened the door. He peeked inside and saw her asleep, snoring. Shutting the door, he returned to the living room and grabbed a Nike duffle bag from out of the living room closet, dropping it before his cousin and uncle.

"Alright, mom's knocked out cold. I'ma get this fire started, so we can burn this shit," Kreon stated to Omar and Jaekwon. Once he got the fire started, he stood upright, facing it while clutching the firewood poker. The flames casted the threesomes' shadows on the wall behind them as they stood side by side, watching the flames lick away at the logs before them.

"Blood, I'm thirsty." Jaekwon headed toward the kitchen.

Kreon and Omar watched, as Jaekwon raided the refrigerator like it was his apartment. Kreon shook his head and hung up the poker, massaging the bridge of his nose. He sat down on the couch, just as Jaekwon was returning from the kitchen with a Pepsi, cracking it open. He sat on the couch beside his cousin and turned on the tv, propping his legs upon the coffee table. Seeing this, Omar looked from Kreon to Jaekwon. Pissed off at how his nephew was disrespecting his sister's home, he stormed over to Jaekwon and smacked his sneakers from off the coffee table. He then shot him an evil eye and clenched his jaws, threateningly.

"What?" Jaekwon sat up, clueless to what he'd done.

"Show some fuckin' respect, that's what!" He mad-dogged him. "Keep yo' fuckin' shoes off the furniture."

Jaekwon thought about what he had done and realized that he was disrespecting his aunt's home. "Oh, my bad, my nigga, Kre."

"It's cool, man, don't wet that shit."

"Here." Omar pulled out Khadafi's priest collar and gave it to Kreon.

Holding the collar at both ends, Kreon stared down at it. He then looked up at his uncle and said, "He's really gone, huh?"

"Yeah," he nodded and gripped his nephew's shoulder, "he's gone."

"He can't ever hurt me again?" Kreon looked him in the eyes, hoping that he'd say yes.

"That's right, nephew. He can't ever hurt chu again... ever."

Instantly, Kreon's eyes became hot and tears ran down his cheeks. Abruptly, he gave his uncle a manly hug. His head shuddered and tears cascaded down his face, shoulders rocking. All the hurt, pain, turmoil, and frustration he had been harboring for years came pouring down his cheeks. He hugged his uncle tighter and went rigid in his arms, sobbing harder and louder. Omar looked to Jaekwon, who looked to not know what to do, so he motioned him over. The thug sat his Pepsi down on the coffee table and embraced his cousin and uncle, in a group hug. They both held tight to Kreon as he cried and cried.

"That's it. Let that shit out, Kre. Let all of it out, nephew." Omar cried himself, his tears running over his lips. He could feel his nephew's pain and hated himself for not being there to stop all of what he had gone through. He felt in his heart that, if he hadn't been so caught up in the streets, he would have taken notice to what was happening to him. He probably could have stopped him from becoming a person with Borderline Personality Disorder but, now, it was too late. Now, he would do everything in his power to help him cope with his mental illness, so he could live a normal life.

After they showed each other love, the fellas burned all their clothing and sneakers. They then showered and got dressed in the clothing from out of the Nike duffle bag. Afterwards, they sat around watching television and chopping it up. Omar glanced at his watch and tapped Jaekwon. They rose to their feet and approached Kreon, who had gotten to his as well.

"You outro, Unc?" Kreon inquired.

"Yeah, I'ma take it in. I gotta see this dude in the A.M." He slapped hands with him and embraced him, kissing him on the side of the head. Kreon made the same exchange with Jaekwon before letting them out. His uncle turned to him and said, "Nephew, burn that." He pointed to Khadafi's collar, which was lying on the coffee table. "We don't need that shit coming back on us."

"Alright." He nodded and shut the door behind them.

Kreon picked the collar up from off the coffee table and chucked it into the fire, watching the flames lick at it. The collar curled up at its ends and turned black. He watched as it incinerated into smoke.

CHAPTER TEN
The next day

Kreon pulled up to his apartment complex and murdered the engine, hopping out of his whip. He slammed the door behind him and came around the back of the vehicle, just as Odette was jumping out. Kreon came to stand beside her and interlocked his fingers with hers, staring up at the building. He narrowed his eyelids into slits and Odette held a hand above her brows, being blinded by the blazing sun.

"This is yo' house, huh?" Odette asked, cracking a smirk.

"Yep, home sweet home. Come on." Kreon walked with her towards his complex hand in hand, removing his keys from his pocket. He opened the door of his home and allowed her to be the first inside, closing the door behind him as he stepped inside behind her. As soon as they entered, they were greeted by the smell of nicotine, Pine Sol, and Clorox bleach. Ella was obviously doing some cleaning around the place. There was proof of this when Kreon and Odette saw the shiny kitchen counter and mopped floor. His mother was wiping off the top of the stove and taking the occasional toke from her square, blowing smoke in the air. The radio played 105.9. She handled the task at hand, singing along with Aaliyah's *Four Page Letter,* appearing to be performing at her own concert. Odette and Kreon smiled, seeing Ella dance and croon, oblivious to the fact that they were her audience. That just made it that much more entertaining for them though.

Kreon told Odette to stay where she was before creeping inside of the kitchen, careful not to make a sound that would draw his mother to his presence. She was singing her heart out, when he came to a stop behind her and placed his hands on her hips. Her eyelids snapped open and she damn near leaped out of her skin when she felt a pair of strange hands. When she whipped around and saw her son, she calmed down a little bit, but her heart was still going mad behind her left breast bone. Eyes still stretched wide open, she placed her meaty hand over her bosom as her chest rose and fell rapidly. Kreon marched over to the radio and turned it off.

"Boy, you scared the living shit out of me," she professed.

"Yeah, I know." He picked up the cigarette that she'd dropped and took a couple of puffs, before passing it back to her. She took it and continued her indulging. She was about to unleash a cloud of smoke but stopped just before she did, once she cut her eyes to the left and found Odette standing at the entrance of the kitchen. It was then that her expression changed to a hostile one and she went ahead to blow out the smoke, polluting the atmosphere with clouds.

"Momma, this is Odette, but I call her O. O, meet my momma, Ella." He smiled, looking between his blossoming love and his mother.

"Hi, how're you doing? It's a pleasure to finally meet chu." She smiled, showcasing all thirty-two of her beautiful white teeth and outstretching her hand.

Ella took the cancer stick from her big chapped lips and blew out smoke into the girl's face disrespectfully, causing her to narrow her eyelids into slits and cough. She tossed the washcloth she'd been using to wipe the stove off with over her shoulder and switched the weight of her body to her other foot, looking the poor girl up and down. Her eyes were evil and her lips was twisted. She'd just laid eyes on her but, already, she didn't like her. For that matter, she didn't really like any woman that entered Kreon's life. This was because she was fearful of them taking him away from her, leaving her to die old and alone. Ever since she could remember, it had just been her and her baby boy, through the good times and the bad times. They may not have had much but they did have one another, and she was terrified of someone coming between that.

Often, she'd find any last-minute reason she could to stop Kreon from seeing a young lady he'd taken interest in. The nigga loved his mother and he didn't want to fall out of favor with her, so he'd often go along with her, ordering him to drop whomever it was he was seeing at the time. He'd never had his father in his life and he'd lost the man that was like a father to him so, naturally, he didn't want to lose his mother. So, he'd coincide with whatever she wanted him to do, like a loyal lap dog.

"Ma, be nice." Kreon lowered his brows and tilted his head, giving his mother the eye like, *don't you start that shit in here.*

Ella sucked on the end of her cigarette and blew out smoke, switching hands with the square. She went on to outstretch her hand, shaking Odette's and giving her a halfhearted smile. "Nice to meet chu, too."

"Good, now I gotta go take a leak." He patted them both on their shoulders and went off to handle his business.

Ella looked down the hallway. As soon as she saw her son disappear inside of the bathroom and shut the door, she started in on Odette.

"What're your intentions with my son?"

"I'm very much in love with your son, Ms. Ella."

"Humph." Ella twisted her lips again and tapped her cigarette above an ashtray, dumping ashes. "My son has a condition, a very special condition. Kreon isn't like any other young man you've ever met. That, I promise you." Her eyelids narrowed as she took another pull from her square, smoke wafting around her.

"What do you mean? His condition?" Her brows furrowed.

"It's not my business to speak of it if he hasn't told you. I'm sure he will when he's ready."

"Indeed."

"Listen, that's my only son, my baby boy. I love Kreon more than I love my damn self. He's as tough as a brown paper bag of old rusty nails, but he has a heart of gold. He's a loving, genuine, beautiful person to those that he loves. I've seen my son broken hearted before and, Lord as my witness, I wish that I could have taken that pain and dealt with it myself 'cause to see him like that killed me. I could have shriveled up and died seeing him in the state he was in." She shook her head sadly, thinking back to her son's first heartbreak.

"Excuse me, Ms. Ella, but you've lost me. What're you getting at?" Her forehead wrinkled.

Ella took the time to dump her ashes out into an ashtray again, before going on to speak. "Be mindful of my son. Be very careful with how you deal with him 'cause God as my witness, if you hurt him." She shut her eyelids and bit down on her bottom lip, tears jetted down her cheeks. She sniffled and made a face, wiping her eyes with the back of her hand. "Just take care of my boy. I can tell he's taken a liking to you and I'd hate to have you hurt 'em. 'Cause should that happen, I'm coming after you." Her moist, pink eyes took on a frightening look. "I'm going to be on you like stink on shit, and I'm not gone let up 'til yo' ass is dead. Do I make myself clear?" Her nostrils pulsated and her chest throbbed. She meant everything she told her; she'd be damned if she did something to her son and she didn't make good on those claims.

"I'm not going to do anything to hurt Kreon. I have feelings for him. I have deep, deep feelings for your son. The last thing that I'm ever gonna do is hurt him. I'd rather he hurt me than I hurt him. That's how deeply involved with him I am." She held her man's mother's gaze, as she stared at her with arched eyebrows and twisted lips.

"If you say so." Ella mashed her cigarette out in the ashtray just as Kreon returned to the kitchen, looking down at his vibrating cellphone. On the screen it said Nigeria, but he wasn't about to answer it, especially with Odette being there.

Ella went on to whip up her son and his guest something to eat. Fried chicken, spaghetti, cornbread, and a salad was on the menu. To wash it all down, she made a pitcher of ice tea with slices of lemon in it. Kreon loved her ice tea. The shit was the bomb to him. He could drink the entire pitcher his damn self. Everyone sat down at the table and ate, shooting the shit. The way Ella and Odette were chopping it up, you would have thought they didn't just get into it earlier. It wasn't that Ella didn't like Odette; she just didn't want her son getting his heart broken again.

After eating, Odette and Kreon kicked it out in the living room on the couch, watching Netflix. Seeing her man dozing off, Odette shook him awake so that he could walk her down to her car. He stretched and yawned, then got up from the couch. Once he had opened the door, she interlocked her fingers with his and led him out onto the tier. Walking towards the steps, they saw people kicking it on the staircase. They were loud talking, smoking, and drinking. These mothafuckas were carrying on like they were at a house party, not giving a mad ass fuck about disturbing the neighbors.

"I'm gettin' tired of this shit, man." A scowling Kreon shook his head. He'd contacted the apartment building's manager, Porsche, about his next-door neighbor, Tranisha, and her guests hanging out on the steps, but shit hadn't changed yet. See, Tranisha didn't take Porsche's word seriously because they were homegirls. Shit, there was a couple of occasions when he'd walk by the door and see

Porsche and her in her unit playing Spades, smoking with whatever dusty ass niggaz they had up in there. From seeing that, it wasn't a surprise to him that old girl wasn't adhering to what she was saying.

"Why don't chu contact your manager about this?" Odette looked at him, curling her arm around his arm and walking towards the staircase.

"For what?" He twisted up his face. "Ain't like her ass gone do shit." He sighed and shook his head again, continuing towards the staircase. Amongst the people on the staircase, Kreon saw this fool, Po. Now, Tranisha had a couple of niggaz she fucked with, but he was the main nigga. All the other dusty niggaz she dealt with were her side niggaz. Anyway, Po and Kreon didn't like one another for shit. Not only did Po contribute to all the fucking noise going on, he kept traffic coming through. Not just from his bitch ass homeboys, but his slinging crack kept crackheads around the building. This brought attention to the location, the location where Kreon also kept the drugs that he sold. The last thing he wanted was the police knocking at his door with a search warrant because of Po's hand to hand serving ass.

There was laughing and loud talk on the staircase. The closer Kreon and Odette walked, the louder and clearer it became to them. When the dark skinned, big lipped nigga that was known as Po looked over his shoulder and saw the couple approaching, he tapped his homie that was sitting beside him. In turn, he alerted the rest of their homeboys and Tranisha. Everything turned silent, smoke continued to waft and mothafuckaz continued to sip from their cups of alcohol, eyes on the couple as they came down the steps. Odette clung tighter to Kreon, and he mad-dogged the niggaz on the steps. They didn't say shit and he didn't either. It was through the eyes that all the communication was done. It became clear that he was willing to take it there if they were. All parties involved didn't want any beef, so they kept shit neutral.

Kreon glanced over his shoulder out of the front passenger side window, beyond Odette. He made eye contact with all the fools on the steps of his apartment building, eyes lingering longer on Po. Throwing the vehicle into drive, he pulled off, knowing that one day he'd bump heads with the thug and all hell would break loose. He only hoped that Odette wouldn't be around when the drama finally popped off.

CHAPTER ELEVEN

"Oh, my God, Kreon, I've never done something like this before," Odette said, grinning. Her back was to Kreon, and he was tying a bandana around her eyes.

"There's a first time for everything," he replied with a smile, pulling the ends of the bandana tight. He then turned her around and grabbed her by her hand, leading her toward the door. Stopping at the coat rack, he took down her purse and passed it to her. Blindfolded, she hoisted the strap of the purse over her shoulder and allowed him to lead her out of the front door.

Kreon opened the front passenger door for her and helped her inside, buckling her up. He then ran around to the driver side door and hopped in, slamming the door shut behind him. He cranked up his car and threw it into drive before pulling off.

"Where are we going?" a smiling Odette asked, feeling around for Kreon's hand. Finding it, she interlocked her fingers with his.

"You'll see; relax, lil' momma, I got this." Kreon smiled at her and kissed her on the lips twice.

***

Reaching his destination, Kreon swung his Pontiac around and backed it up. Afterwards, he hopped out of the car and stashed his keys in his pocket, running around to the passenger side. He opened the door and took Odette by the hand, helping her out of the vehicle and slamming the door behind her. He brought her around to the rear of the Grand Am and popped the trunk, lifting it up. He rummaged through his trunk, while Odette had her back to him. Although she didn't know where she was, she was trying to feel out her surroundings, hoping to get clues to where she was.

A smile etched across Odette's face, feeling the warmth of the sun shining down on her through the openings of the trees leaves. She held up her hand to the golden light and smiled harder, enjoying the warmth that the sapphire in the sky provided. Odette drew her hand back once she heard the chirping of birds and heard them flapping past her, loose feathers drifting in the air. She looked to her left, feeling the bird flying across her path. Next came the splashing of water and quaking. It became apparent to her that there were ducks nearby, which brought her to the conclusion that she was near a body of water. Excited, she clapped her hands and jumped up and down, turning her head toward Kreon.

"Oh, my God, Kreon, you brought me to a lake? What do you have planned? A picnic?"

"Ummm, maybe," he said with a smile, setting everything up for their picnic.

"I'm so excited, babe. A guy has never taken me out on a picnic before." Hearing him walk past her and stop at the trunk, she looked to him. Smelling a tantalizing aroma, she sniffed the air and licked her lips. "Smells banging. What chu brought for us to eat?"

"Mind yo' business, nosy." He capped with a smile, taking something out of the trunk and kissing her on the cheek.

"Can I take this blindfold off now?" she asked.

"Nope."

"Aww, come on. Let me steal a peek." She made to remove the blindfold.

Kreon stopped what he was doing and looked to her, saying, "O, if you remove that blindfold, I'll shoot chu in one of them big asses titties of yours."

"Please, please, please, please," she begged like a little girl, holding her interlocked hands up.

"Not just yet. Gimme a minute, Slim, and I'll take it off."

With that said, Odette impatiently waited for Kreon to finish what he was doing, so they could start their date.

"Alright." Kreon stepped behind Odette and untied the bandana. He took a deep breath and yanked it from off around her eyes. Instantly, Odette's eyes lit up and the biggest smile had formed across her face. She took in the scenery, seeing the ducks in the lake and the setting her boo had made. Laid out on a blanket not too far from the water was boxes and containers of Popeye's chicken, plastic utensils, paper plates, napkins, and a bottle of wine, which was sitting in a bucket of partially melted ice. Besides this, there were a pair of elegant glasses and a carton of peach Minute Maid juice.

"Oh, my God, Kreon, this is awesome. You even got my favorite chicken. I fucking love Popeye's." She kicked off her flip flops and ran toward the blanket. She got down on her knees and made her a plate of wings, red beans and rice, biscuit, and corn on the cob. Picking up the wing, she bit into it, shutting her eyelids and smiling. The crispy chicken was delicious. "Babe, this is the bomb.com, take a bite. Here." She sat the plate down and held up the wing for her boo to take a piece, holding her hand beneath it to catch any crumbs. He took a bite and chewed, grinning at her. Afterwards, the couple ate, laughed, and talked. They poured up a glass of wine and a glass of peach Minute Maid for Kreon.

Odette laid back against Kreon's chest, taking the occasional sip of wine while she and her man stared out at the lake while watching the ducks fly to and from off the surface of the water, sprinkles of water splashing onto the surface of the water.

"This is nice, babe. This is real nice," Odette said, admiring the scenery of the place that she and Kreon had taken up. "I must admit, I never took you as the romantic type." She smiled, looking over her shoulder at the dazzling smile of the conqueror of her heart.

"I'm not," Kreon responded while stroking her chin gently with his thumb, staring lovingly into her eyes. "You brought it outta me, lil' momma." At that moment, that tantalizing smile of hers stretched across her face that made him putty in her hands. Kreon swept the individual braids from out of her face and pulled her closer, kissing her slow and passionately.

Kreon went to pull back, but she grabbed him by the collar, holding him in place and kissing him again. They smiled at one another. He licked his lips. "Mmmmm, I can taste the wine from yo' lips."

"I can taste that peach juice from off yours." Odette licked her lips also. She then took in her surroundings, marveling everything presented before her eyes. It all seemed so peaceful and tranquil. It was nothing like South Central, Los Angeles. Here, it was sunshine and the uncanny sounds of Mother Nature, while the hood had the familiar sounds of gunfire and police sirens. The two places differed greatly in appearance as well. Yeah, it was safe to say that this little spot was like her utopia. "Mmmmm, I can get used to this." She took another sip of wine and continued to take in all the sights.

When she said this, Kreon took his eyes from off her and took in the full scope of the surrounding area. "What, this place?"

"Nah," she turned around and looked at him, seriousness bleeding from her eyes, "being with you."

Kreon presented her with the biggest smile that he had ever shown in his entire life. They sat down their respective glasses, and Odette aggressively peeled off his clothing. He tried to help her take off hers, but she refused him, opting to slip off her panties instead. He let it slide, figuring that she may have been insecure about her body. By this time, the sun had begun to set, so Kreon, clad in just in boxer briefs and Chuck Taylor's, popped the trunk and got out a couple of T-light candles. Opening the door of his whip, he popped in a mix CD of love songs that he had speakers. Grinning, he looked through the windshield and saw Odette with her thighs squeezed tight. He could tell she was fiending for the dick then.

Next, Kreon grabbed a Bic lighter from out of the change tray and hopped out of the Grand Am. He slammed the door shut and walked to the blanket where his love awaited him. He placed the candles all around the blanket and lit them, one by one. Afterwards, he removed his boxer briefs and engaged Odette; they had hot, steamy sex right there by the lake, beautiful candle light, and music serenading them in the night. As they were both climaxing, the lights of the candles flickered out and the tenth song on his CD ended.

Kreon laid on his back, staring up at the sky and smoking on the electric vapor cigarette that Odette had brought along for them to indulge in. His arm was wrapped around her and her head laid against his chest, hand playing with the hairs there. She laid there listening to him tell her about his upbringing. He didn't say much. Other than that, it was rough. He mainly focused on his mother and how she was growing up. He had good things to say about her, but he also had some bad things to spill as well.

"She didn't tell me that my pops wasn't my old man 'til I was twenty-five. That shit fucked me up, O. Imagine thinking that the cat that you thought was yo dad for all of those years turning out not to be." He took the electric cigarette from his lips and allowed a fog of smoke to roll off his tongue. His eyes turned glassy and wetness formed in his eyes, but he blinked back tears.

"My mom..." he heard his voice crackle a bit, so he shut his eyelids briefly and cleared his throat. "My mom was the first woman to ever break my heart. I mean, how can a woman not know who the father of her child is? That's some hoe shit to me, letting niggaz run up in you raw like that. That's a female that doesn't have no respect for herself." He shook his head pitifully and continued to smoke.

By this time, Odette had tears sliding down her face. Sniffling, she rose from off his chest, leaving him facing her back. Kreon's forehead crinkled and he sat up from where he was lying, wondering what the matter was with her.

"What's good, O?" he asked concerned, hearing her weeping.

"There's something I have to tell you, and it may make you look at me different." She glanced over her shoulder at him, face shiny from her tears. The moon was slightly illuminating her.

"What is it?" he inquired, passing her the cigarette.

Odette took the cigarette and took a pull. Blowing out a gust of smoke, she quickly gathered her wits and began, "Like your mother, I didn't know who Marquise's father was. I had an affair with my high school sweetheart." She looked at him to see if his facial expression had changed, but it hadn't. Now, he had scooted closer to her and started caressing her back soothingly. She continued telling the story. "At the time, my marriage with my husband was rocky, but that's not an excuse. I know that doesn't make it right. I made an idiotic mistake that put, not only my health, but my marriage at risk."

Odette's entire body shuddered and she bowed her head, big teardrops falling from her eyes. Kreon continued to caress her back, telling her that she didn't have to finish telling him the story, but she needed to let him know. She was fearful that he wouldn't want her anymore, figuring that she was a straight up hoe, but she had to tell him. She wanted him to accept her regardless of her past and her flaws. That was the only way that she was going to know that he truly loved her.

"I let Carlos know what I had done and he beat my ass, but he insisted on me not getting a paternity test. As far as he was concerned, Marquise was a Lopez and he didn't want to hear anything else about it." She took a pull of the cigarette and passed it back to him. "Once Marquise got about two years old, we knew that he was my husband's. He had his texture of hair and the extra nipple that Carlos has on his pecks. Plus, he looked like a mixed kid. Donald, my high school sweetheart, was a brother. That was the only way that we knew for sure..." she trailed off and broke down, crying her eyes out. Sitting the electric cigarette aside, Kreon embraced and hushed her, rubbing his hand up and down her back to comfort her.

"Shhhhh. It's okay. It's alright, everything is gonna be just fine," Kreon consoled his lady, like only he could.

Odette wept a little longer before she pulled away from Kreon, looking up at him with a tear-streaked face and snotty nose.

"You don't... you don't look at me any different?" she stammered, wiping her face with the back of her hand and sniffling.

"Nah." Kreon shook his head no. "You know who lil' man's pops is; my mom doesn't know who mine is. Besides, my moms allowed me to think that some other nigga was my old man when he wasn't; you didn't do that with your seed." He swept her braids out of her face and caressed her cheek with the side of his hand affectionately. "I gotta ask though, did you ever tell Donald that Marquise may have been his?"

"Yeah, I told his ass." She shook her head shamefully, sniffling again. "Mothafucka had the nerve to excuse me of trying to trap him."

"Trap him?" He lifted an eyebrow questioningly.

"Yeah. He was a rapper. You heard of the Dope Money Klique?"

"Fa sho'. I never listened to their music though."

"Well," she swallowed the spit in her throat, "he was down with the crew that they had signed, The Hoodfellaz. He was making a little money, but the nigga wasn't getting it like that. Hell, he still stayed in the hood; I wasn't trying to trap him. He didn't really have shit."

"Where is he at now?"

"He's still in Connecticut, far as I know."

"Y'all still talk?"

"Every now and again, he'll hit me up."

"Were you still fuckin' with dude after you and hubs separated?" Odette gave him a look that confirmed it. She didn't even have to say shit.

If she still fuckin' with dude, it has to be on some booty call shit. If they still choppin' it up every now and again, then that means he comin' through smashin' whenever. If we get together, she could fuck around on me with him. I ain't takin' that chance. Slim gone have to ax that nigga, or her and me can't be. Fuck that!"

"Peep this, O. If you tryna build somethin' witta nigga, then there's somethin' that you gotta know. My lady can't be friends with exes, nor have male friends. 'Cause if me and you beefin', then that shoulda to cry on becomes a dick to ride on, ya griff me?" She nodded yes while hugging him, the side of her face pressed against his chest. Her face was wet, but she wasn't crying anymore. "First things first, you gotta delete all yo' exes outta yo' phone and un-friend that nigga Donald on all social media. Matter fact, bang homie line and tell 'em not to hit chu up 'cause you gotta man."

Odette took his head from his chest and looked up at him. "Ain't no need for me to do that 'cause we don't talk like that. For real, like I told you, every now and again I hear from him."

Like I said, a mothafuckin' booty call, Kreon thought to himself.

"Cool. The rest of what I said goes, if you tryna fuck with a nigga. If not, then leave it be. What's it gone be?" Odette didn't say a word; she whipped out her cellphone and deleted all of her ex-boyfriends' contacts. Seeing this caused Kreon to smile. He never wanted a girlfriend because he knew of all the games bitches played. You know, fucking around with their baby daddies or their exes, making the nigga they with look stupid as a mothafucka. He didn't trust nobody, but he really didn't trust females. The way he saw it, they were just as foul as the niggaz out there in the streets. But since Odette had deleted all her exes from her cellphone, it showed him that she may be different than the broads he heard about and dealt with.

"Done." She smiled at him once she was done were her deletions. "Now, it's yo' turn."

"Cool. I only got one broad in my phone and that's Nigeria." He showed her Nigeria's name in his contacts and then deleted it. Odette smiled after he deleted homegirl's name out of his cellular. Afterwards, he took her by both of her hands and looked her directly into her eyes, saying, "Listen, O, if I'm with you, then I'm with you. You ain't neva gotta worry about a nigga fuckin' around on you. I don't expect nothin' from you that I don't expect from myself. That's just my get down. All I ask is that you stay loyal, faithful, and neva make me feel like anotha nigga comes before me. That means if I say cut a nigga loose, then you cut 'em loose, no questions about it, ya griff me?"

Odette nodded and said, "I promise to never make you feel like another man comes before you. All I ask of you is to be loyal, faithful, treat me like a queen, and to love me unconditionally. I want chu to love me like the air you breathe."

"You are the air I breathe, O."

The moon shined brightly above the couple. Odette's eyes pooled with tears and she gave him that smile that he adored so much. At that moment, the lovers leaned forward and kissed romantically.

Odette and Kreon kicked it on the blanket, staring up at the stars and talking a little longer. Afterwards, they got dressed, packed everything up, and rolled out.

"Bae, can we stop by the liquor store? My sister wants a couple of Black & Mild's." Odette looked to Kreon from the passenger seat, rubbing her hand up and down his thigh.

"Smooth," he replied, staring straight ahead through the windshield. It was dark out, so the light flickered on and off his face as he sped through the city's streets. He turned up the volume on Future's *Karate Chop*. Odette went right behind him and turned it down. His forehead crinkled and he looked to her. She was turned to him, eyelids narrowed and lips puckered up for a kiss. He smiled and gave her a quick kiss before focusing back on the streets before him.

"Ol' spoiled ass," Kreon claimed, chuckling.

"Nigga, yo' ass is spoiled, too," she chuckled and playfully shoved him. He shoved her back and they laughed. Shortly thereafter, she laid her head against his shoulder and hooked her arm with his, shutting her eyelids and smirking. "Bae?"

"Sup, slim?" he asked, still focused through the windshield.

"I love you."

"I love you that much more, Mocha."

***

"Man, this mothafucka packed, can't even finda park," Kreon said, circling the liquor store's parking lot. They were here to grab the tobacco products that Odette's sister requested.

"Why don't chu just double park? I can run right in," she suggested.

"Nah, I don't want chu goin' up in there alone. Niggaz out here be on some bullshit."

"You sure? I can run in and run right out."

"Trust me, slim." Kreon brought his car to a stop and narrowed his eyelids, looking ahead and seeing a Mazda 626 pulling out a parking space. A smile stretched across his lips, causing his cheeks to rise. "There we go. Homeboy leavin' right there." He took his hand off the steering wheel and pointed at the vehicle that was leaving, making Odette look. As soon as the car had left the space, he was pulling up in it.

Kreon took his keys out of the ignition and stashed it inside of his pocket. He opened his door and hopped out, interlocking his fingers with Odette and walking toward the entrance of the liquor store. They pecked on the lips and kept on about their business, swinging the arms of their interlocked fingers back and forth. The bell chimed as soon as the couple crossed the threshold into the liquor store. They laughed and chopped it up as they searched through the store together, gathering the junk food they wanted to sneak inside of the theater to eat that night.

It wasn't long before Kreon came galloping out of the liquor store laughing, giving Odette a piggy back ride. She had a sour apple straw hanging from out of the corner of her mouth. One arm was slung across Kreon's neck and she was clutching a brown paper bag in her hand. Her other hand was at her back, smacking his back like he was a real horse running along.

"Whoa, Nelly! Whoa!" Odette called out like a cowgirl. Kreon slowed down as he neared his car, making noises like a horse.

"Hahahahahahahahaha!" Kreon doubled over laughing.

"Hahahahahhahahahaha!" Odette laughed as he let her down to the ground. "That was fun."

"Really? Well, next time... next time, you play the horse. Matter fact." He switched hands with the brown paper bag that was in his possession and turned her around, making to climb upon her back. He stopped himself short and they both laughed again.

Odette pulled the sour apple candy straw from out of her mouth and chewed what was left in her mouth. She then pulled Kreon into her and kissed him deep and passionately. He pulled away and wiped the extra spit from the corners of his mouth, smiling at her lovingly.

"Come on, we don't wanna be late for the movie." Kreon opened his door and hopped inside; Odette was right behind him. He had just cranked up his ride and made to back out when a charcoal-gray Pontiac Trans-Am with a fading Eagle on its hood pulled to a screeching halt behind him, leaving him no room to get out of his parking space. The music coming from the Trans-Am was so loud that it caused the late model car's body and windows to vibrate.

"Fuck is he doin?" Kreon frowned up. "I know this mothafucka see me tryna get out." He looked to Odette and then back over his shoulder through the back window. At that moment, the driver's door of the Trans-Am swung open and a white dude stepped out, spitting on the ground. He was dressed in a leather jacket, tight blue jeans, and worn, brown leather cowboy boots. When he hopped out of his whip, his lady wasn't far behind. She was a blonde whose dark hair was pushing up her dyed hair from its roots. Although it was dark out, she was wearing shades, a jean jacket, and skirt. She ran her fingers through her hair as she chewed gum.

"Bae, don't trip, let's just wait. I mean, they're just running into the liquor store; how long could they be?" Odette tried to reason with him.

Kreon's head snapped around to her; his eyebrows arched and wrinkles formed around the beginning of his nose. He was looking at her ass like she was a coward. "Man, fuck alla that!" He went to honking the horn like a mad man while staring at homeboy through the sideview mirror, watching as he and his girl headed for the entrance of the store.

"Come move yo' mothafucka car, Billy! Fuck you expect us to get out?" he yelled out of the window of the driver side window, repeatedly honking his vehicle's horn. Although he didn't know homeboy's name that was pushing the Trans-Am, he called all the Caucasian men 'Billy' that he wasn't familiar with.

Honk! Honkk! Honkkk! Honkkkk!

Kreon relieved the horn and stared at old boy through the sideview mirror. The cock sucka threw up the middle finger as he proceeded towards the establishment, one hand on the hip of his woman.

"Baby, please, let's just chill. I don't wanna ruin our night," Odette pleaded.

Kreon wasn't trying to hear that shit though. He was enraged, seeing red and steam was rising from off the top of his head.

"Nah, babe, this mothafucka ain't about to ruin our night. He just gone have to move his shit, it's as simple as that." He went back to honking the horn and calling out of the window. "Move yo' mothafuckin' car, bitch!"

The white cat turned around, face twisted in anger. His girl, thinking that he was about to fight Kreon, grabbed him by the arm, but he snatched away from her. "Fuck you! I'll move my fucking car whenever the fuck I feel like it, ya prick!" Spit jumped off the thin lips of the white stud's five o'clock shadowed face. Afterwards, he turned back around to go inside of the store, and that's when that nigga Kreon snapped.

"Oh, this nigga gone act like we ain't even here? Like we mothafuckin' invisible? Oh, okay, he done fucked with the wrong one!" A pissed off Kreon popped his trunk and opened the driver side door. He turned to hop out and Odette grabbed his arm, staring at him with pleading eyes.

"Babe, please. If you truly love me, just-"

"Fuck off me." He snatched away and hurried around to the rear of his car, throwing open the trunk. He rummaged through the stuff he brought for the picnic until he found what he was looking for: a tire iron. He lifted up the tire iron before his eyes and smiled evilly, licking his lips. He slammed the trunk of his car, just as Odette was hopping out and slamming the passenger side door closed. She pleaded for him to stop, but he wasn't listening. Homie was too far gone. He was in the zone.

"Didn't I tell you to move yo' shit?" Kreon barked at the white dude, pointing the tire iron at him. "Didn't I? Huh? Well, it's time to pay the mothafuckin' piper, homeboy!"

"Kreon, stop! Stop! Stop!" Odette hollered at him, tears dancing in her eyes.

The white cat yanked away from his girlfriend and went running after Kreon. He was too late though because he was already working on his car, cracking his windows and creating cobwebs out of the glass until they eventually broke. The shards of glass rained down on the surface and resembled twinkling diamonds under the soft lights of the parking lot. Once Kreon was done with the windows, he stared wailing on the sideview mirror until it broke off and fell. Next, he started punching holes into the door and hood of the Trans-Am. By this time, the white dude was unlocking his trunk with his key and lifting it open.

"Kreon, stop it!" Odette continued to yell, looking back and forth between her lover and the white dude who was now reaching inside of the trunk of his whip. Her heart was pounding so hard that she could hear it inside of her ears. Her blood pressure was through the roof, too. She knew this because her head had started hurting and she felt a migraine coming on.

"Bitch ass mothafucka," Kreon spat flames, madness danced in his pupils, and his eyebrows sloped. He swung the tire iron down hard on the hood and on the side of the Trans-Am, denting it up. Next, he stabbed the sharp end of the tire iron into the front tire of the vehicle, bursting it. The tire hissed and slowly deflated, tilting the Pontiac Trans-Am to one side.

"Oh, my God!" Odette's eyes stretched wide open, seeing the white stud come from the trunk of his car with a chrome .9mm held at his side. The beautifully crafted weapon had the design of two snakes zig zagging across one another and the handle of it was pearl. "Kreeeooon!"

Kreon froze stiff and looked up, breathing hard. His chest rose and fell as he stared down the white dude. He tilted his head down, glaring up at the man that he had a problem with.

"Go ahead! I'm not afraid to die! Shoot! Shoot me, bitch!" Kreon roared at homeboy, who pointed his .9mm straight at his chest, ready to spit death at him.

"Get the fuck away from my ride!" the white cat barked while turning red, he was so angry. Creases were on his forehead and his nose was scrunched up.

"Brent, just let it go, baby; let's just get outta here!" the white cat's girlfriend pleaded, clinging to his arm. Brent looked like he was weighing his options, but Kreon kept egging him on.

"Shoot me, nigga, shoot! Ol' hoe ass nigga!" Kreon raged, eyes turning glassy as he clenched his jaws while putting the bone structure of his jaws on display.

"Fuck you!" Brent frowned and gritted, pulling the trigger of his lethal weapon.

"Noooooooo! Nooooooo!" Odette hollered out, terrified by the danger that her lover faced.

Bloc!

The tire iron spun around so fast that it looked like a small helicopter propeller. It deflected off Brent's gun, knocking it out of his hand and making the shot go wild. The tire iron clanked to the ground of the parking lot and Kreon charged after his threat. Once he reached Brent, the nigga swung on him and he ducked it. Coming back up, Kreon cracked him in the jaw and he fell to the right, head deflecting off the trunk of his Trans-Am. He slid down to the ground, back against the back tire of the vehicle.

"Stop, get off him!" Brent's girlfriend called out to Kreon. By this time, he was standing over her boyfriend, pummeling his face with his fists and bloodying his knuckles. Police car sirens wailed in the distance. Kreon didn't acknowledge this because he was in a zone whooping Brent. The white stud's head whipped from left to right with each punishing blow. Kreon had menacing eyes and was gritting his teeth, swinging with all the hatred in his heart.

The white girl jumped on his back, but he flipped her over on the ground. Turning back to Brent, he held the roof of his Trans-Am with both hands and began stomping that ass out. His victim's body twitched violently each time Kreon's Chuck Taylor came down upon his battered, bleeding face.

"Kreooon!" a voice rang out from behind the young man, and he felt someone grasp his shoulder firmly. He whipped around with his fists raised, about to knock flames from whomever it was who had put their hands on him. His face was twisted with hostility, but that expression quickly drained from his face seeing that is was Odette behind him. He blinked his eyelids repeatedly, like he was awaking from a dream. Suddenly, the sounds of the police car sirens flooded his ears and he realized exactly where he was. He looked around, seeing bystanders surrounding him and Brent laid up against the back tire of his car, moaning in pain. His girl was kneeled beside him, inspecting his injuries.

"Kreon, come on; we gotta get out of here!" Odette continued to pull on him. Finally realizing that his freedom was up for grabs, he took off running with his girl following closely behind. When they hopped into his Pontiac, the car sitting before them was backing out of the parking space. As soon as it was gone, Kreon sped out of the parking lot.

Kreon sped through the streets, coming past police cars that were heading in the direction that he had just came from. His chest was heaving up and down from his breathing heavily. His face was shiny from sweat brought on by the assault he'd launched on Brent. When he looked to Odette, she was looking at him like he was crazy.

"You okay, Mocha?" Kreon asked concerned. He leaned over to touch her and she scooted away from him, not wanting him to touch her.

Fuck she lookin' at me like she doesn't know me for? Like she's scared of me? he thought.

Kreon frowned and shrugged, brushing off Odette's attitude. He focused back on the streets and continued to drive.

35 minutes later

Kreon pulled up outside of Odette's crib and murdered the engine of his whip. Looking at his hands on the steering wheel, he noticed that his knuckles were bloody for the first time. A line creased his forehead and he took his hands from off the steering wheel, looking at him as if they didn't belong to him. Hearing the passenger door being opened, Kreon looked to Odette and saw her getting out of the car. He grabbed her by her arm and she stopped, looking over her shoulder at him.

"Hold up. Where you goin'? You ain't tryna give a nigga a goodbye kiss or nothin'?" Kreon complained.

"I don't know about you getting no kiss."

"Why not?" He frowned. "Close the door. I'm tryna chop it up witchu."

Odette had a look on her face, like she was weighing her options. Coming up with her decision, she took a deep breath and her shoulders slumped. She shut the door and settled back in the passenger seat.

"Now, what's the matter?"

"What's the matter? Are you fucking serious Kreon?" Her brows furrowed. "You snapped, back at the liquor store. It was like a switch had gone off in your head and you became someone else. You beat the living shit out of that man back there. I thought you were going to kill his ass. You scared the hell out of me. I have never seen you like that before."

"I griff you, but homeboy had it comin'. You seen 'em talkin' that shit and not tryna move his car. Shit, that white mothafucka pulled a strap out on me; he coulda took my life! I owed him that one!"

"You almost killed him, bae. In front of all those people too," she said as she shook her head. Little momma couldn't help seeing her man in a jumpsuit and shackles being escorted to a prison bus. "If that would have happened, then I would have been coming to see you behind the wall. Then, there would have been no telling when I would have been able to see you again." Her eyes welled up with tears. "Baby, I just… I just… I just couldn't go on living life wondering if I was ever going to have you hold me in your arms again."

"I griff you. And you're right." He popped the glove box and took out a handful of Church's chicken napkins. He started wiping the blood from off his knuckles, revealing the small cuts and the bruises on them. "I lost it back there. It was like I had gone mad, like I had left this world for another one… one that was all my own." He stared ahead, wide eyed, thinking about how he had set it off on Brent back at the liquor store's parking lot. "I was blinded by my rage, and all I could think about was beatin' that bitch ass nigga to death," he scowled and clutched his fist so tight that veins formed around it.

"Kreon, you need to check into an anger management program and get yourself some help."

"I'm good, O. A nigga gotta lil' temper but, other than that, I'm cool. I don't needa go to no place like that."

"You do." She opened the door. "And I'm afraid I cannot see you anymore until you get yourself together." She hopped out of the car and so did he. Standing up outside of the driver's door, Kreon looked on, as Odette ran toward the door of her home. He called out behind her, but she kept on running. Seeing that she wasn't going to respond, he just stood there watching, as she opened the door of her house and slammed the door behind her.

"Hey, Missy, you had a good time?" Shonda asked from the couch where she was watching the tv show, *60 Days In*. She rose from off the couch and approached her, smiling. "Well, how was it?" she asked of her date once again, anxious to get the details. Her little sister seemed to have been smitten with this Kreon she had heard so much about, so she wanted to know what it was like to kick it with him.

"Oh, I had a wonderful time," Odette rummaged through her purse until she found the two Black & Mild's that her sister had asked her to get for her on her way home from the lake. "Here you go, sissy pooh." She passed her the tobacco products and she took them. Shutting her eyelids, Shonda pulled one of the Black & Mild's back and forth beneath her nose, inhaling its fine scent. She was enchanted by the thin cigar's unique aroma.

"Thanks. Now, about your date."

"I'm sorry, sis. Can I tell you about it later? I'm tired as hell. I just wanna get Marquise and shoot to the house."

"Okay. Are you sure everything is okay?" Her face slightly balled up, seeing the perplexed expression on her sibling's face.

"Yeah, everything is good. I promise, I'm going to hit chu up tomorrow and tell you all about it," she mustered a fake smile. "Where's my baby at?"

"He's back there in his room asleep."

"Okay. Are you spending the night?"

"No. I'm gonna go home and finish watching *60 Days In*, while I indulge in this here fine cigar," she replied as she held up one of the Black & Mild's.

"I heard that. Well, thanks for watching little man for me, sis," Odette said as she pecked her on the cheek and seen her to the front door, before heading to her son's bedroom.

***

Once she'd kissed Marquise goodnight, Odette took a shower and took care of her hygiene. She hated wearing her bra and panties to bed, so she threw on a wife beater and pajama pants. Next, she turned on the tv and flipped through the channels, but she couldn't find anything worth watching. Giving up, she turned off the flat-screen and laid across her bed. Her thoughts drifted to Kreon and what happened that night. She really hoped he would do like she had asked because she really wanted to see him again. But, she knew if he didn't, she more than likely wouldn't see him again. The nigga had a temper, a bad temper. This made her weary of him. Because who was to say that he wouldn't flip out one day and beat her ass like her husband used to? Shit, for all she knew, if they were to move in together, he could lose his cool and abuse her son because he pissed him off.

Odette laid in bed with her eyelids shut, waiting for sleep to take her away. Right when she was drifting off, her cellphone rang and vibrated. Its screen lit up from where it was on the dresser. Odette peeled her eyelids apart and looked to her cellular. A line etched across her forehead, wondering who it was. Her curiosity got the best of her and she peeked over at the display of her device, seeing Kreon on it. Next, she fell back upon the bed, staring up into the darkness and contemplating on whether she should answer her cellphone or not. While she was doing this, her cellular continued to vibrate and ring continuously.

In her heart of hearts, Odette believed that Kreon was the man that she had prayed for that day in church. She could feel it in her gut that he was the man that God had sent to her. She'd hate to think that, by cutting him off, she'd be ridding herself of her one true love. He could be the one that she was destined to be with, and she wasn't trying to fuck that up. Sure, he'd lost his temper and beat the dog shit out of that fool in the liquor parking lot, but that was what his ass got for giving him a hard time. Hell, the mothafucka had pointed a gun at him. He could have killed him. Now that she thought about it, she couldn't put Kreon at fault for what he did. If the shoe was on her foot, she probably would have done the exact same thing that he had done.

Not wanting to derail fate, Odette decided to throw her concerns to the wind and answer her telephone. She looked up at the ceiling and said, "Lord, I hope this is the man that I been praying that you bless me with every night. If this is yet another throwaway nigga, I'm going to have a bone to pick with you once I get to heaven." Odette picked up her cordless telephone and took a deep breath. It rang three more times before she pressed 'talk' and brought the receiver to her ear.

"Hello?" she spoke into the cordless.

"Sup with it, slim?"

"Nothing," she mumbled as she made herself comfortable in bed and slid underneath the covers.

"You were debating on whether or not you were going to answer the phone, huh?"

"No. I had just jumped out of the shower when I heard the phone ringing. As a matter of fact, I'm drying off right now," she lied.

"Unh huh," he replied, not believing a word she'd said. "Look, I thought about what chu said tonight and I am gone see about getting into an anger management program. I coulda fucked around and beat that nigga to death tonight. I mean, that beef wasn't worth me losin' my freedom over, ya griff me?"

"Yeah, I griff you," she chuckled. She'd never get over his slang.

"Besides, if all it takes is me goin' to anger management to keep someone as wonderful as you are in my life, I'll stay in that mothafucka forever, for real," he claimed.

Hearing this made a smile spread across Odette's face. It was nice to be in love with someone that thought the world of you.

"Are you for real, Kreon?" she asked, smiling and playing in her braids like she always did when she was feeling his conversation.

"Sheiiit, is a pig's pussy pork?"

Odette busted up laughing and said, "Boy, you are too much, I can't take you."

Odette and Kreon's conversation continued throughout the night, until they found dawn sneaking upon them. Even then, they kept right along talking until Odette fell asleep. Kreon didn't hang up though. He listened to her soft snoring as she slept, until he eventually fell asleep on the phone with her.

CHAPTER TWELVE
That night

Young Kreon laid in bed on his side, sound asleep. A dark figure with a cane, holding something in his hand, appeared in the doorway. He took a sip from what was shaped like a tall can and stood where he was, seemingly watching the youngster sleep. Suddenly, Kreon's eyelids snapped open and he sat up in bed. He looked to the digital clock and saw that it was 12:05 A.M. When his eyes went to the doorway, he found Khadafi standing there taking casual sips from his golden Old English can of beer. Through the outside light shining in the window, he could make out half of him: his Kufi, his gold rimmed glasses, and overcoat. Kreon was scared, not knowing what he was going to do to him. Especially with him just standing there, studying him like he was a dissected frog on the table in class.

"Did... did I do something?" Kreon stammered, fear creeping inside of his heart.

Khadafi downed the last of his beer, crushed the can in his palm, and burped loud and nasty. After dropping the ruined can off into the waste basket, he wiped his mouth with his fist and addressed his son.

"Get dressed, we're gonna go on a lil' ride."

"Where?" He frowned.

"What I tell you about askin' me so many damn questions, boy? Get cha shit and get dressed, so we can go. I'll be waiting in the car." He turned his back on him and walked off down the hall, body weight leaning to one side for the support of the cane. With the command given, Kreon hopped out of bed and got dressed lightening quick. The little nigga didn't even bother to put on socks. He just stuffed his chubby feet into his sneakers and grabbed his jacket on his way out of his bedroom door.

When he emerged out of the house, he found Khadafi sitting behind the wheel of his army green, late model Plymouth. He took a deep breath before hurrying down the steps, wondering where he was being taken. He wasn't going to ask where they were going again, for fear of getting his ass beat. Jumping into the front passenger seat, Kreon slammed the door shut, stealing the attention of his old man.

"Gotdammit, watch how you slam my door, junior. Shit, lil' nigga." He frowned.

"My bad. Sorry."

"It's alright, hold this." He passed him a fresh Old English can that he'd procured before leaving the house. The young man held the can like it was disgusting, his eyes studying it. Khadafi threw his arm over the back of the headrest of the passenger seat and looked over his shoulder. His eyes were focused out of the back window as he sped out of the driveway in reverse, careful not to hit any cars. As soon as he reached the street, he threw the car into drive and took off.

Kreon fidgeted around nervously in the front passenger seat, glancing at his father who was taking the occasional sip from his Old English can. He snapped his head back around once he found him staring at him. A creepy smile spread across his five o'clock shadowed face, showcasing his beige teeth and the silver tooth he had on the side.

"You want some?" he asked, outstretching the can in his direction.

"No." He looked to the floor, afraid to look him in the eyes.

"Gone take a sip, put some hair on them lil' nuts of yours." He nudged him with the can repeatedly until he gave in, taking the can within his meaty hand. He took the can to the head and his face frowned up, tasting the bitter, cheap beer.

"Ahhhhhh, that's my boy." He took the can from him and ruffled his beading hair. He then went back to drinking his alcoholic beverage. When an old Marvin Gaye song came on, Khadafi turned up the volume and told his son that he'd met his mother at the Trinity Park dance when the song first came out.

Kreon listened to the music for a time before clearing his throat, finally gathering the courage to ask the question that was on his mind.

"Ummm... uhhhh... where... where are we going?" he asked, timidly.

Khadafi had just taken a swallow of beer and nodded, wiping his mouth with the back of his fist. *"Mmmmm, good question... you know them movies of mine you like watching so much?"* He cracked a wicked smile once he noticed Kreon lower his head shamefully, constantly fidgeting with his fingers. *"It's okay, son, 'least you aren't a faggot. I know you like pussy like your old man,"* he chuckled. *"Now, as far as where we're going, we're going to get cho dick wet."*

"My... my dick wet?" Kreon's forehead furrowed.

"Yes, we're going to get chu some pussy, son. When you getta bitch excited, she gets wet. Hence da term gettin' yo' dick wet. Damn, boy, fa you to always be runnin' around in the streets, you sho' is as green as lettuce." He smiled and took another gulp of the alcohol.

Kreon swallowed the lump of nervousness in his throat, visualizing what he saw the men in his father's dirty movies doing to women. The chicks in the video seemed to be doing a lot of screaming and hollering, with pleasure plastered on their faces. From what he gathered, they seemed to be enjoying what was being done to them and the men that were humping them appeared to be too. Still, his young mind couldn't quite comprehend what was happening; the idea of engaging in such an act disturbed his adolescent stomach. He thought he was about to vomit.

Kreon found his heart banging against his chest bone, he became so nervous. He knew what his old man had in mind and he didn't want any parts of it. Looking at the movies from time to time was okay, but the idea of having sex terrified him. Before long, he was blinking his eyelids rapidly and breathing huskily.

"Yes, sir, we're gonna get cho lil' dick wet." Khadafi reached over and massaged his son's shoulder, happy about him about to drop his load that night. The event would be as epic as prom night to him, or so he hoped. "Hell wrong witchu?" He frowned up, wondering what the fuck was going on with his boy.

Abruptly, Kreon threw open the front passenger side door and jumped out of the car, while it was still in motion. He hit the surface hard, rolling and scraping himself up. Wincing, he peeled himself up from off the street and got upon his feet. He limped away as fast as he could, looking over his shoulder frightfully. He was already moving fast but, when he heard the wheels of his father's Chevy Lumina screeching to a halt, he sped up.

"Come here, boy, come here!" Khadafi called after him as he rounded his car, coming after him as quickly as he could on that bum ass leg of his leg.

"Haa! Haa! Haa! Haa! Haa." Young Kreon occasionally looked over his shoulder as he broke down the street, the sidewalk looking like the belt on a treadmill he was moving so fast. His chest inflated and deflated, as he took in gulps of air through his lungs. Coming upon a short gate, he grasped its railing and leaped over it hurriedly. He cleared the front yard on his way to the backyard, passing an old Mazda 626 in the driveway on his way to the back. He squeezed his way through the opening of the chained black iron gate, looking over his shoulder and seeing his *father's shadow on the driveway's surface. Having oozed through the gates into the backyard, he darted across the lawn past a German Shepherd on a lengthy chain. When he looked ahead, he saw the lights inside of the house whose backyard he was in; he turned around to see the dog's house. That's when he heard the locks of the back door being unlocked. Kreon swiftly stashed himself inside of the dog house and squeezed his eyelids shut, putting his hands together in prayer.*

"Please, God, make me invisible so that he can't see me. Turn me into a bird so that I can fly far, far, far away, please." Tears came bursting through his eyes and his body began to shudder. He heard his father and who he assumed was the owner of the home he was hiding out in, talking as they neared his location. He peeled his eyelids open and looked up to see the Shepherd sniffing, his wet tongue licking him. He pushed the dog's face away and saw two sets of legs standing outside of the dog house; he recognized one of them as his father's. Khadafi leaned down and peeked inside. His face twisted in hatred and he motioned him out. The youth scooted to the back of the dog house, avoiding his reach.

"Boy, get cho ass outta there 'fore I beat cho mothafucking ass, come here!" he roared, swaying his hand back and forth while trying to grab his little ass.

"No! No! Noooooo!" he screamed and sobbed, snot bubbling out of his nose.

"Alright, you must think I'm playing witcho lil' fat ass!"

Bunk! Buunk! Buuunk!

Khadafi kicked the entire dog house over and grabbed his son by the back of his neck. Squeezing it and causing him to wince, he walked him toward the gate. He gave a weak smile and a nod to the house owner, continuing his way.

Present

Kreon shot up from where he was lying on the sofa bed from his nightmare, in a cold sweat. His heart was raging inside of his chest as he planted his socked feet on the floor, running his hands down his face. He took a deep breath and his shoulders slumped. When he brought his head back up, he was teary eyed. Hearing the faint sound of snoring, he looked down at the floor and discovered his cellphone. Its screen was still lit and Odette was on it. The time on it read two hours and fifteen minutes. That's when he realized that he'd fallen asleep on the phone with her. As soon as he picked his cellular up, he placed it to his ear.

"Hello? Helloo?" Kreon spoke into the receiver. All he got in response was Odette's snoring. He disconnected the call and sat his cell down on the coffee table. Throwing his head up, he looked at the ceiling, talking to God Almighty. "With all the shit that I've been through, you'd think I'd get a fucking break! One single fucking break, but nooooooo, I've gotta wake up from fuckin' nightmares, feelin' all depressed and shit, like always! Fuck!" He punched the sofa, repeatedly. Afterwards, he snatched his pill bottle from off the side of the coffee table and looked at it. It was halfway full of pink pills. "Waste of my fucking time!" He threw the bottle and it deflected off the wall, landing on the floor. Kreon grabbed his cellular again and speed-dialed his psychologist. He knew he wouldn't answer because it was afterhours, so he was going to leave him a message.

As soon as the answering machine picked up, Kreon started in. "Fonzworth, these fucking pills aren't workin'. What the fuck, man? It's like my condition is getting worse than before. Check this out; either get me some fucking meds that work, or I'm finding me a new fuckin' shrink!" Disconnecting the call, he looked up in time to see his mother walking into the living room.

"What's your problem?" Her face balled up, seeing her son so irate.

"You my fuckin' problem, ma!" Tears flew down his cheeks as he pointed his finger. "It's because of you and your fuckin' abusive, drunk ass boyfriend that I'm like this! Was the dick that good, ma? Huh? Was it that good that you'd allow a man to abuse your only child, your first fuckin' born? Huh? Please, tell me 'cause I seriously wanna fuckin' know!" he said, putting on his clothes and stashing his .38 on his waistline. He'd already put on his Chuck Taylors.

Ella made a hideous face. It seemed as if she couldn't stop the tears from pouring down her face. She snorted back snot and swallowed the lump in her throat. "I... I loved him."

"You loved him? You fucking loved him?" He frowned up and pressed his hands against his chest. "More than me, huh? More than yo' own flesh and blood?"

"No." She shook her head, holding her hands to her face.

"Obviously, you did, obviously, 'cause I'ma fuckin' head case because of it now!" he screamed at her. His face was so wet from tears that he looked like he'd been splashed with a bucket of water. The abuse from the man he thought was his father all his life among the other hardships he experienced had left his mind a fucking mess. The world had chewed him up and spit him out. Crazy? Maybe, but he wasn't born that way. Nah, those mothafuckas made him that way.

"I'm sorry, Kreon, I'm sorry," she sobbed. "I made mistakes in raising you, some really bad mistakes. Mistakes I wish that I could take back and I'm sorry." She grabbed the sleeve of his hoodie as he paced the floor, causing him to stop. "Tell me what I can do; tell me what I can do to fix this! Tell me what I can do to make this up to you. Tell me, then it's done!"

"You know, ma, all I wanted you to do was love me. That's all I ever wanted, that one thing." Tears rolled down his cheeks unevenly, as he held up one finger.

"But I did love you, baby." She cupped his face, staring into his crying eyes.

"I don't wanna hear that shit." He pried her hands from off his face. "You waited until I was twenty-two to tell me that Khadafi wasn't even my father. All the years I took his unwarranted punishments and neglect, and the mothafucka wasn't even my pops."

"I know, baby, and I'm sorry. I'm so, so sorry, Kreon," she cried, hands together like she was praying. "Please forgive me."

Kreon narrowed his eyelids. "Forgive you, ma? Forgive you? Do you have any idea the damage that has been done behind you letting that miserable fucking bastard stay with us? Do you!" his shouting startled her, causing her to jump. "I can tell you a million times about the crazy shit that goes on inside of this mind of mine, and you still won't be able to fathom how it is to be in my shoes, to wake up every goddamn morning hating any and everything about yourself. I'm confused all the time. There's, like, a ka-trillion things racing throughout my mind. I wish that I was dead every fucking day. What's worse is I gotta deal with this sickness in my head all alone. All by myself, ma." He wiped his tearing eyes with a curled finger.

"You don't have to face it alone. I got cho back." She wiped her tearing eyes with the palm of her hand.

"No, you don't, ma! You never have!" A line creased his forehead. "You haven't been to one appointment that I had with my therapist. When I showed you the paperwork that I was given on my illness, you didn't even fucking read it. You just tossed that shit aside." He threw the imaginary paperwork aside like he saw his mother do. Hearing this, Ella bowed her head shamefully. What he was saying was indeed true. She was too busy gossiping on the phone to pay what he'd given her any attention. "Right. So, tell me how I'm supposed to believe that you care about me? Let alone love my looney ass?" Snorting, he made his way towards the door and pulled it open. Looking over his shoulder, he said, "You wanna know something, ma? I get up every morning and stick my pistol in my mouth." He patted the bulge on his hip. "I try to think of a reason to not kill myself and, every morning, that reason is O. I love her, ma, and do you know why?"

Ella was shuddering, crying, and wiping her eyes. "Why?"

"Because she gave me something you or anyone never has... love." And with that, he slammed the door shut on his way out, rattling the portrait of a younger him and his mother on the wall. It fell to the floor and cracked down the middle, symbolizing that their bond had been broken. Ella shut her eyelids and fresh tears jetted down her cheeks.

***

Kreon stepped out onto the tier of his apartment complex, shutting the door behind him. His mother had managed to royally piss him off. He was wishing Tranisha and them bitch ass niggaz she kept around were kicking it out on the staircase, just so he could pull that thang off his waist and light the front of that bitch up. Fortunately, for them, they weren't outside. Seeing this, he decided to take the time to clear his head by putting some Black & Mild smoke up in the air. He was coming down the steps to go to the liquor store to cop the tobacco product he had in mind, when his cellphone rang and vibrated inside of his pocket. He'd just stepped down to the landing when a line etched across his forehead, wondering who it was that was calling him. Once he pulled his cellphone out of his pocket and saw his uncle's name across the screen, he immediately answered it.

"What's up with it, Unc?" Kreon spoke into his cellular, carrying his husky form towards his Pontiac. He was chewing his tongue and listening to what he was being told, when he suddenly stopped and brought his head up, a concerned expression crossed his face. "I'm on my way there now." He disconnected the call and ran to his car, jumping behind the wheel and pulling off.

***

Kreon let down the windows inside of his car and inserted his mix CD. He searched through the tracks until he found the song that he was looking for. A moment later, Tupac's *Dear Momma* erupted from the speakers, rattling the trunk of his vehicle.

And even though I act crazy
I gotta thank the Lord that you made me
There are no words that can express how I feel
You never kept a secret, always stayed real

Kreon nodded his head and said the words along with Tupac, eyes turning glassy. He couldn't help thinking of all the ups and downs he and his mother faced coming up. They'd been through some of everything that you could think of together. It was always just the two of them, their little family.

Although his mother had made some major mistakes raising him, there were good things that she did for him too. She used to take him go-kart racing, to amusement parks, buy him the latest video games, and systems, clothes, Jordans, jewelry. Hell, she even bought him his first car.

Kreon remembered the late nights he and his mother stayed up watching movies, playing Spades, Twister, Life, Back Gammon, Monopoly, etc. He and his mother had good times together, really good times together. Still, he had to take the bitter with the sweet in life. And his mother was always around to deal with the bitter... he'd never forget that.

Kreon had gotten so depressed that, at eleven years old, he tried to kill himself. He emptied every pill bottle that there was inside of the medicine cabinet into his mouth and laid down in the bathtub, shutting his eyelids and waiting to die. An hour had gone by, but he wasn't dead. He did, however, have the worse stomach cramps he'd ever had before. The youth tried heaving the drugs up, but the contents of his stomach wouldn't budge. That's when he said fuck it and picked up an ink pen. He forced it down his throat twice before his lunch and what was left of the pills came splattered on the floor.

Afterwards, Kreon sat in the corner of the kitchen with vomit at the corner of his mouth and the front of his shirt. Weak and teary eyed, he sat in the corner staring at nothing, looking spaced out and shit, his chest rising and falling as he breathed. He would be found later by his mother, who had been lying across her bed talking to homegirl the entire time.

Kreon sat there listening to his mother inside of the other room, staring ahead at nothing like he'd been since he sat down in the corner.

"Girl, hold on, Kreon is too quiet in here; let me see what he's doing," Ella said, loud enough for her son to hear her from the kitchen. He heard her get from off the bed, calling out her name as she wandered throughout the house, checking bedrooms. Stepping inside of the bathroom, her calling of her only son's name fell silent. He figured she'd discovered the empty bottles of over the

counter drugs that he'd taken in an attempt to commit suicide. He believed this because he heard her gasp and say, "Oh, my God," before dropping an empty pill bottle and come running from out of the bathroom.

Ella ran into the kitchen and stopped dead in her tracks, seeing her son sitting in the corner looking like a mess. Instantly, she started crying and talking to Lord Almighty.

"Oh God, oh God, Ooh God, don't let this be happening, please don't let this be happening!" Ella dropped her cordless phone and it deflected off the floor, landing on its side. "Why? Why? Why? Whyyy, Kreon, why?" Her hands trembled at the horrifying sight. She thought for sure that he was dead because he wasn't moving and he had a vacant look in his eyes. Getting down on her knees, she leaned closer to him and used her thumb to force open each of his eyelids, seeing if he was alive. Afterwards, she placed two of her fingers to his neck to check his pulse. That's when she realized that he was alive. "Oh, thank you! Thank you, Lord Jesus!" She looked up at the ceiling and gave The Man Upstairs her appreciation for letting her son be alive. "Kreon, Kreon, Kreon, Kreon!" She smacked him on his cheek repeatedly. The last smack came a little harder than the others, but it got him to come to his senses. She knew this because he moaned and looked at his mother lazily, as she held him by the lower half of his face and caused his lips to pucker up.

"Yessss.... yes, momma?" Young Kreon moaned again, head lulling about.

"Are you okay, baby boy?" Ella asked in a panic, tears steadily sliding down her face.

"My... my stomach hurts..." he trailed off, moaning once again.

"It's okay, I can fix it. I can fix this." She gave him a quick hug and kiss. When she broke her embrace, her son *puked again, plastering the floor with a nasty looking goop. This caused her to frown, knowing that he still had some of the medication in his stomach. She figured that she could call 9-1-1 and they'd send an ambulance. The E.M.T.'s could pump what was left of the drug from her son's stomach.*

Ella was about to dial 9-1-1 but, then, she thought about Child Protective Services getting involved and trying to take her son away from her. With this in mind, she hung up and got her baby boy to his feet. She hurriedly slipped on something and grabbed her keys, running out of the house. She burned rubber from off the residential block and stopped at CVS, buying these pills that would help Kreon throw up the last of the pills. Outside in the parking lot, Ella stood behind her son, rubbing his back as he threw up back to back. Tears were running down his cheeks as he continued to hurl up, not only the drugs, but whatever he'd eaten earlier that day.

"Momma, what did you gimme? It feels like… it feels like I'm finna throw up my insides." Kreon threw up again. His contents of his stomach splattered on the ground, some of it getting on his sneakers.

"It's okay, baby. It's okay. It's just something to make sure that you get everything outta your belly is all," she explained to him, watching him dry heave for a minute. "You think you got everything?"

"Y… yeah." He nodded, wiping his mouth with the back of his fist.

Ella looked around to see if anyone was watching them. There wasn't. "Come on, let's get outta here," she said as she grabbed him by his hand and hurried him over to her Ford Explorer Sport, slamming the door shut behind him. Next, she hopped in behind the wheel of the enormous truck and slammed the door shut. She laid back in her seat, staring up at the ceiling as tears cascaded down her cheeks. Sniffling, she looked over at Kreon and he was staring out of the windshield at nothing, face wet from crying. The boy was involuntarily fidgeting with his fingers.

"Kreon." Ella leaned into him, rubbing her hand up and down the back of his neck. "What is it that made you wanna kill yourself? What happen to you?" she questioned with concern bleeding out of her eyes. He was quiet, staring ahead and fidgeting with his fingers, like he'd been. "Talk to me, baby. Give me something," she pleaded.

Kreon shut his eyelids briefly and sniffled, crying some more. "I... I feel sad all of the time, momma. I... I hate myself. I hate being me... oh God, I don't want to live anymore," he broke down, spilling buckets of tears and shuddering like he was in cold, rainy weather. Seeing this, Ella wrapped her arms around him and kissed him on the top of his head. Teardrops fell from off her chin as she cried.

Jesus, Lord, my child is only eleven years old! Why does he want to die? He's still just a baby... my baby, Ella thought, rocking her child back and forth in her arms. She took one hand from off him and wiped her nose with the back of her hand swiftly. She sniffled and stared out of the windshield, listening to her son's sobbing and feeling his body tremble against hers. "Momma's gonna get chu some help, sweetheart, I promise. We're gonna get through this."

Ella took Kreon to see a psychologist at UCLA hospital. After a few sessions, the doctor concluded that he had manic depression, which they later found out was Bipolar Disorder. Both diagnoses would turn out to be wrong though. Anyway, he was given anti-depressants and pills for his anxiety. The youth took the drugs that the psychologist gave him, but they didn't seem to work. Most of the time, he still felt sad, lonely, and depressed. Still, he continued to take his medication in hopes that it would keep his emotions in check, but it didn't.

Kreon had mood swings. I mean, horrible mood swings. He could go from happy, mad, sad, and depressed in a matter of minutes. He hadn't noticed in years that this was happening. In fact, he thought that it was normal. It wasn't until he started getting involved with the opposite sex that they pointed out to him how his emotions flipped flopped. He'd be loving, caring, and affectionate one minute, and distant and not wanting to be touched in the next.

It wasn't until he'd gotten into his late twenties that he was diagnosed with Borderline Personality Disorder. He was familiar with it because he'd read up on all kinds of mental illnesses when he was reading up on the one that he believed that he had.

***

Kreon plucked the ticket from the automated machine and the hand rose. He drove around the parking complex of Kaiser Hospital, looking for a space to park. Finding one, he parked and smacked the ticket on the dashboard. He removed his safety belt and snatched his keys, hopping out of the car. As soon as he slammed the door shut, his cellular went off and he grabbed it from out of his pocket. He glanced at the screen and saw his mother's name present. Holding the cellphone in his hand, he stared at it as it continued to ring, contemplating on whether he should answer it or not. His thumb hovered over the green phone sign. He was about to press it and answer the call but changed his mind at the last minute, opting to end the call.

"Fuck her. She pissed me off," Kreon scowled and stashed the device in his pocket. Pulling his pants back upon his ass, he mobbed toward the elevator lobby, eager to see what the situation was with his uncle.

Tranay Adams

CHAPTER THIRTEEN

Kreon ran down the west wing of Kaiser Hospital, his sneakers screeching on the waxed linoleum. His head swayed from left to right, looking in each of the rooms that he passed. Finding the number of the room that he was looking for, he darted to it and entered calmly. As soon as he crossed the threshold, he found his uncle laid up in bed. A nurse had just handed him a cup of water and some pills. Tossing them back, he washed them down with the water. Afterwards, he crushed the cup with his hand and tossed it into the waste basket. With that out of the way, the nurse went on about her business.

Omar's eyes were red webbed and moist. The hair on his head was wild and unkempt. From the expression on his face, it was obvious that something was wearing down on his mind heavily. The man looked as if he had the world on his shoulders. Kreon's eyes shot to his uncle's hand. It was trembling. This let him know that he was in dire need of nicotine. A Newport would get his mind right at that moment.

"Sup with it, Unc?" Kreon slapped hands with his relative and embraced him, patting him on his back. He then sat down on the chair nearest to the bed. A line crossed his forehead, wondering what was going on with him. "Yo', what the fuck happened?"

"I'm stressed. I'm stressed the fuck out, man. I mean, for real, for real." His eyes never looked to his nephew. He was staring ahead with a far out look in his eyes. It looked like he was in a trance. While Kreon was listening to him, he pulled out the pack of Newport's he'd requested before he went up to see him. Having pulled the curtain closed, he took a cigarette out of the pack and lit it up for him. Sitting back in his chair, he watched as he took the first puff of his cancer stick. Instantly, his nerves began to settle, or so it appeared to his nephew. "Somebody is talking."

Kreon's forehead creased and he said, "Talking on what? Spit that shit out."

Omar finally looked to his nephew. Blowing smoke from his nostrils and mouth, he said, "That thing I did for you."

With that, Kreon blew hot air and slid down in his chair. He massaged the bridge of his nose and shook his head. His uncle was talking about his murdering Khadafi on his behalf. Suddenly, his head snapped up and he looked up at him. "Wait a minute, I know you aren't thinking that I…"

"Nah!" He shook his head.

"Excuse me!" a voice rang out, a scowling doctor snatched the curtain open. He mad-dogged Omar, looking like he wanting to put those paws on him. The O.G. mad-dogged him back, like 'Nigga what's cracking?' "You can't smoke in here, man. You gotta put that out!" Omar ignored him and went on smoking his cigarette like he didn't hear what the fuck he said or didn't give a fuck about what he said. Either way, he was giving him his ass to kiss. "You hear me, man?" With that said, Omar blew the toxic smoke in his face.

Kreon looked back and forth between his uncle and the doctor. "Yo, Unc, fallback, we gotta 'nough on our shoulders to deal with."

The O.G.'s hateful eyes lingered on the doctor a time longer, before he dropped the square into the cup of water on his nightstand. The ember of the cigarette hissed when it splashed against the surface of the liquid, sizzling out.

"Fuck out my face, nigga!" Omar spat at the nigga in the lab coat that was getting on his last goddamn nerve.

The doc's eyes lingered on him a while longer, challenging him. This was to let him know that he wasn't afraid of his ass. Having had enough of being in the old gangsta's presence, he drew the curtain closed and went on his way, talking that shit as he went.

"Punk ass nigga."

"What?" Omar grumbled. He threw the sheet off him and made to get out of bed, but his nephew held him back. "Ol' busta ass, nigga, you must don't know I'ma thug and I'll strangle yo' mothafucking ass up in here!" His nostrils flared and his chest heaved violently. He struggled against Kreon's arms before eventually settling down and throwing the sheet back over himself.

Seeing that his uncle had somewhat settled down, Kreon pried him for some information. "You said somebody speaking on that murda, right? Well, who all knows about it?"

"You, me, and Jaekwon." He looked him dead in his eyes. Each name mentioned sounded like a .44 Magnum revolver going off. This caused Kreon's stomach to turn and his heart to drop. Because if he didn't tell and his uncle didn't open his mouth, then that only left one nigga to point the finger to: Jaekwon.

Kreon blew hard and ran his hands down his face. He was stressing now. "How did all of this come about? How you know that Jaekwon is telling?"

Without saying a word, Omar reached underneath his pillow and pulled out a manila envelope. He looked his nephew in the eyes as he smacked it down on the nightstand, slowly removing his hand. Hurriedly, Kreon snatched up the envelope and opened it, pulling out the documents inside. His heart raged inside of his chest and he gasped, looking back and forth between the signed affidavit and his mother's brother. It was true. It was right there in black and white, Jaekwon's statement. He recounted Khadafi's murder that night to The Boys. All Kreon could do was shake his head, pitifully. Jaekwon was the weak link in their family, a mothafucking cheese-eating rat. They had never had one of those until now.

"How did you get this?" Kreon passed the envelope back.

"I gotta nigga in my back pocket that's connected to some higher ups. That's all I can say," Omar told him. "Now, I'm guessin' the only reason why our black asses ain't locked away is 'cause these devils are lookin' to bury me alive, nephew. They want some more shit on me. A murder is cool, but there's a chance that I can come up from under that with the right attorney. Besides, they don't have a body either. For all they know, Jaekwon is just talkin' outta his skinny ass, so he won't see a 6x9, ya griff me?" Omar and his nephews dropped Khadafi's body off at a crematorium, where it was burned to ashes by a mortician that he kept on salary for situations like the one he was tangled up in.

"This shit is crazy." Kreon took a deep breath and ran his hands down his face. "Why the fuck this nigga just flips? I mean, what's his reasonin'? Not that it matters. I'm just curious." He pulled up a chair and sat down on the side of the bed. His uncle had dropped a real bomb on him and his shoulders were heavy. He and Omar had committed a murder with his cousin and, now, he was trying to use it against them, like he wasn't an accessory to it as well.

"The Ones popped his ass with two birds and a banga," Omar reported. He then went on to give Kreon the rundown on what had happened the night Jaekwon had gotten picked up with the gun and drugs. "So, yeah, the bitch ass nigga made a deal with them people."

"Who put chu on to 'em?" Kreon leaned forth, resting his elbows on his knees and steeling his fingers under his chin.

"Nobody. I peeped how the mothafucka was actin' that night chu came by to re-up," he confessed. "He was a lil' off, sweatin' and lookin' all around and shit. The nigga was paranoid. I wasn't for sure, but I had my suspicions, which is why I sicced my guy on 'em. He did an investigation and discovered that the lil' weasel was garglin' the Feds dick and balls. That cock sucka was bending it over and bustin' it wide open for 'em."

Kreon sat up in the chair and leaned his head back, looking up at the ceiling and taking a deep breath. Bringing his head down, he looked to his uncle and said, "What's the next move?"

Suddenly, Omar grew quiet. Looking him dead in his eyes, he said, "Nephew, family or no family, Blood gotta go." He made his hand into the shape of a gun and pulled the imaginary trigger. "I just can't be the nigga to do it, ya griff me? I'd be the numba one suspect if somethin' happens to bitch-boy."

"No doubt," Kreon said. "I'll do it." This made his uncle's forehead deepen with lines. He narrowed his eyelids. It was hard for him to believe that his nephew was so willing to knock off his own cousin. Even he didn't want to do it, and the slime ball had ratted him out.

"You serious?" Omar looked him in the eyes for any signs of hesitation. There wasn't any.

"Straight up, we gotta take care of our own, right?" Omar nodded his understanding. Kreon rose to his feet, slapping hands with his uncle and kissing him on his forehead. "I'ma handle this shit for you, don't even trip." He tapped his fist against his chest and walked out of the room.

A couple of days later

The large, thick, iron double doors opened outward with a loud squeal, and then Drennen came strolling out casually, taking a gander at his surroundings. He had a haircut so fresh that he still had hair inside of his ears. He wore his signature glasses and crucifix, along with a button-down shirt. His shirt was tucked into his slacks, which had a snakeskin leather belt that held them up on his waist. His pants were starched to a crisp, lying over some black leather shoes. These shoes were polished to a shine so fine that he could see his smiling face in them. The nigga looked like a corporate thug in his attire, especially with the gold Rolex watch adorning his wrist. Drennen hoisted his sack over his shoulder and placed a jeweled hand over his brows, peering up at the beaming hot sun. He narrowed his eyelids and a smile stretched across his lips. Homie was happy to have his freedom. It had been a while since he'd been out in the world and he planned to take full advantage of it. After taking a deep breath, the smile stretched further across his face. Although the air had smelled something awful, he welcomed it into his lungs. Having been incarcerated, he realized that it was the smaller things in life that mattered.

Drennen was about to begin his journey back to Los Angeles, when something far off in the distance grabbed his attention. Sitting his sack of belongings down on the ground, he removed his glasses and fogged its lenses with his breath. Whipping out a handkerchief, he flapped it out and used it to clean his glasses. He slid them back on his face, adjusted them, and narrowed his eyelids. Looking ahead, he spotted a red stretch Hummer on 28-inch chrome rims that was driving in his direction. He massaged his goatee, wondering who it was on board the sexy machine, but no one came across his mental. Drennen hoisted his sack over his shoulder and began his trek, when the humongous vehicle came to a halt before him, freezing him in his tracks.

The hummer was still and quiet. Instinctively, Drennen went for his waistline, but then he remembered he'd just been released from prison and he wasn't strapped. Having realized this, he dropped his hand to his side and waited to see what was going to happen next. There was a prolonged silence, and then the back door opened and two bikini clad women slid out. One was bronze and the other was caramel, but they both were startlingly attractive. The moment that nigga Drennen saw them, he felt his dick nudge at his zipper. The caramel girl smiled and waved at him, batting her long eyelashes flirtatiously. While she was doing this, her counterpart ducked off inside of the vehicle and pulled out a sign, holding it to her chest. Drennen took a good look and saw that the sign had his government scrolled across it. Seeing this, he went on to approach the ladies. They ducked off inside and waited for him to climb in behind them. He did.

The bronze beauty broke out the champagne flutes and began pouring up the glasses. While she was doing this, caramel took the liberty to roll up a bleezy of that Loud. Having licked the blunt closed, she swept the golden flame of the lighter back and forth beneath it to seal it shut. She took a couple of puffs from the end of it and passed it to Drennen, who indulged in it as well. Before he knew it, the bronze girl was passing him one of the flutes. They all toasted to his freedom and bomb ass sex.

Drennen threw back what was left in his flute and set it aside. One of the girls gave him a black wooden box with golden locks on it. He took the time to pop the locks. Once he opened the lid, he found two golden envelopes, one of which was fatter than the other, and a Ghost Gun. A Ghost Gun was a firearm completely untraceable. It was expensive too, ranging anywhere from $5,000 to $10,000 dollars.

Switching hands with the blunt, the first thing Drennen opened was the fat golden envelope. Once he had thumbed through all the bluish green Benjamin Franklins inside, he closed it back up and set it back inside of the box. Next, he opened the other golden envelope and pulled out the letter, which he unfolded and read. His eyes moved from side to side, as he fed his mind the information on the letter. Drennen folded the letter back up and took the lighter from caramel. He set the end of the letter on fire and watched it curl up and turn black, as the flame ate away at it. He stared at the burning piece of paper with a serious, concentrated look in his eye.

Next, he held down the button that operated the back window, descending it. The limo was speeding, so he could hear the noise of other speeding vehicles blowing past. Tossing the burning letter out of the window, he rolled it back up and went back to smoking. Drennen picked The Ghost Gun up from out of the box, checking its magazine and its sighting. Satisfied with the craftsmanship of the lethal weapon, he placed it back inside of its placement and shut the box. He sat the box beside him and, when he looked up, his hooded eyes saw the bronze girl was tearing open the golden foil of a Magnum condom and the caramel one was swiftly unbuckling his slacks. It wasn't long before his hardness was being pulled from its confinement, and the latex was being rolled down his shaft. The bronze girl slipped off her bikini bottom and squatted over his erection. Taking it by its shaft, she guided it inside of her warmth, hissing like a snake as it filled her up. Once she'd found her rhythm, she went ham on the dick, while her homegirl sucked on the ex-con's nut sack. Drennen threw his head back and his eyelids fluttered like a butterfly's wings, enjoying his homecoming gifts. His ears were flooded with the sensual moans of the women, the suction noise from his sack being sucked, and the noisy leather seat of the limo as he was being rode.

Continuing to ride her fuck-buddy, the bronze girl took the blunt that was pinched between his fingers and took drags. She polluted the air with smoke as she worked up a sweat. Drennen laid back, looking through narrowed eyelids with a smirk plastered on his lips. He was in heaven now. Omar broke him off with a nice chunk of change, set him up in a fully furnished apartment, gotten him clothes, shoes, and even a gun. All he had to do was take care of whatever business that his homeboy had for him and this nigga was financially straight. For now, he would enjoy himself because once he went to see his people and got his personal business in order, he was going to take care of the business that was assigned to him.

Tranay Adams

CHAPTER FOURTEEN
That night

"Damn, girl, this shit feels good than a mothafucka," Kreon said, eyelids shut. He was lying on his stomach in bed, with Odette straddled on him. Her glistening hands were at work, massaging hot baby oil into his flesh. The way he was moaning and licking his lips, anyone listening would think that he was getting the blow job of his life. "Ssssssss, shit, Mocha, you went to school for this shit or somethin'?"

She chuckled and said, "Nah, I've had plenty massages though. I'm just applying what little I know to what I'm doing here."

"Well, you doin' one hell of a job, slim."

"Thanks, handsome." She smiled halfheartedly, continuing to work her magic on his meaty back.

"Mmmmmmm." A smirk stretched across Kreon's lips and he turned his head upon his chin, facing the black tint of the 55-inch flat-screen tv. He peeled his eyelids open and saw the pitiful expression across Odette's face, as she massaged his back. The skin on his forehead bunched together as he wondered what was the matter with her. "Sup, Hersh?"

She looked up at his reflection on the television and weakly smiled, shaking her head and saying, "Nothing." With that said, she went back to massaging his back.

"Nuh unh, we not finna start that shit." He tapped her leg and she climbed off him, allowing him to roll over on his back. She crawled over to him and laid her head against his chest, playing with his chest hairs as her moist eyes stared up at his. While she was doing this, he was rubbing his hand up and down her back. "What's up, baby? Talk to yo' nigga. Let 'em know what's goin' on."

Odette took a deep breath before she went on to tell him what was on her mind. "Your mother doesn't like me."

"What?" He frowned and sat up. "What makes you think that?"

"The first time we met." She went on to tell him about her and his mother's first encounter.

"Are you serious?" He frowned further.

"Yeah." She nodded fast, tears falling unevenly down her cheeks. He took the time to wipe them away with his finger and thumb.

"Come on, we going to holla at mom's." He sat up on the couch bed and slipped on his clothes. She got dressed too, sliding her small feet into her black Air Force Ones last. Once he'd gotten fully clothed, he took his lady by the hand and led her to his mother's bedroom. Standing before it, he could hear the television from the other side; his mother was watching *16 and Pregnant*. "That tv loud as a mothafucka on the other side of this door," Kreon said to no one.

"Hold on, girl," Kreon overheard his mother say to whoever she was on the cordless telephone with. "Who is it?" she called out, loud enough for her son to hear through the door.

"The nigga you pushed outta yo' pussy," he responded back to his mother.

"Babe," Odette scowled and nudged him. "Don't talk like that to her. She's your mother."

Kreon looked at her and shrugged, before turning his attention back to the door.

"Watch cho mouth and what do you want?" his mother asked.

"I needa holla at chu, old lady."

"About what?"

Kreon didn't even bother answering; he turned the knob and pushed opened the door. He found his mother snuggled under the cover with the cordless cradled to her ear. The blue illumination from a 40-inch flat-screen tv flickered on her person, as she talked on the phone and took the occasional pull from her Newport, polluting the air with smoke.

"Ma, I needa talk to you for a minute," Kreon told the woman that had given him life.

"The way you look, it must be pretty goddamn serious."

"I'd say it was."

"Girl, lemme call you back. Nah, everything is alright. My son just wants to have a word with me. Oh, alright." She disconnected the call and sat the cordless on the nightstand, continuing to indulge in her cigarette.

"Ma," he began, hands together, shutting his eyelids briefly. "I don't need you checkin' every female that I bring through here. I'm not tryna wife up every skirt that chu see me with. I'ma grown ass man. I can handle myself. You gotta stop treatin' me like I'm some poor, defenseless goddamn kid!"

Odette looked from her man to Ella. She was staring at him and taking tokes from her cancer stick, like she didn't have a care in the world. She could feel the tension in the air with how heated Kreon was growing in his conversation with her. Since she'd known him, she knew how explosive his anger could be and she was fearful that he may end up putting his hands on his mother.

"Baby, you think you could bring your voice down just a-"

"Not now, O." He whipped his scowling face around to her, giving her a look that said, *your ass had better be quiet or else.* He then turned back around to finish addressing his mother. "Back to what I was sayin', you owe O an apology."

"For what?" Ella sat up in bed and tapped her square, dumping ashes into the ashtray beside the bed on the nightstand.

"For threatenin' to harm her if she breaks my heart."

Ella glanced at Odette and then back to her son, eyebrows arching. "I wasn't just talking outta my ass, I meant what I said. If she hurts you, then I'm gonna-"

"O isn't going to break my heart, ma. 'Cause I don't have one to break. There ain't shit here." He smacked his hand up against the left side of his chest, clapping the fabric of his shirt against his peck.

"Baby, you-"

"Apologize." He gave her a stern look and his nostrils flared.

"But-"

"Now!" he snapped, startling her and causing her to shut her eyelids for a moment.

Swallowing the ball of hurt that had formed in her throat from her son talking to her the way that he was, Ella went on to peel her eyelids back open and apologize to Odette. "I'm sorry." She sniffled and her eyes twinkled.

"O, do you accept my momma's apology?" he asked, eyes lingering on his mother.

Holding on to Kreon's arm and looking his mother in the eyes, she said, "Yes."

"Okay, good." He went on to address his mother. "Momma, here's somethin' you needa understand, I'm your goddamn son; I'm not your man! So please, please, pleeease, stop actin' like I am! If you tired of bein' single, then find yo' self a man, 'cause I can't be it. I'm someone else's man, alright?" He stared her dead in her eyes. She was glassy eyed. Not saying a word, she continued sucking on the end of her Newport, creating smoke clouds. His words had hurt her, but she wasn't about to let him see that they did. Ella didn't need to respond; the look on her face told him that she'd heard him loud and clear.

"Babe, come on." Odette tugged on his arm. Now, she felt bad for bringing her concerns to Kreon. She didn't expect him to wild out on his mother like that.

Kreon was standing there staring at his mother while her eyes were focused on the tv, acting as if he wasn't even there. Her eyes had pooled with tears and she knew that if she dared to blink, tears would slide down her cheeks. "Come on." She tugged his arm again. He lingered in the bedroom for a time longer staring at his mother, before walking off with his chick. As soon as he shut the door behind him, tears came running down her mother's eyes. She sniffled and the tears continued to flow.

***

Kreon came out of the apartment holding Odette's hand. He froze where he was when he saw Po and his homeboys loitering on the staircase, getting drunk and high as usual. That chicken head ass bitch Tranisha was out there, too.

Seeing the strained look on her man's face, Odette's face balled up. "Bae, what's wrong?" she questioned with concern. Looking from him to the niggaz politicking on the steps, she realized why he had frozen in his tracks. "Aye, we can just chill inside of the house until they leave."

With that, his head snapped in her direction and he narrowed his eyelids threateningly. Her suggestion caused him to angle his head to the side and look at her like she lost her goddamn mind.

"I ain't locked up, so I'll be damned if a nigga dictates when and if I leave my mothafuckin' house. Let's go." He squeezed her hand tighter and moved forth, feeling at ease being that he had that steel on his hip. Kreon must have said excuse me a dozen times as he came down the staircase, making his way through the bodies on the steps, nearly knocking over plastic cups and bottles of dark liquor. Kreon and Odette had just stepped down to the surface, when that nigga Po grabbed a handful of her ass and squeezed. Odette jumped and her eyes lit up. Furious, she whipped around and smacked flames out of Po's ass. The impact whipped his head around and he held his stinging cheek, which had a red imprint on it.

"Nigga, don't chu ever put cho mothafucking hands on me!" She wagged her finger in his face. Her eyebrows were arched and her lips were twisted.

"Bitch, you musta lost yo' mothafucking mind puttin' yo' hands on my man!" Tranisha and her man's homies all hopped up ready for the bullshit, but that nigga Kreon put an end to that shit really quick.

In a flash, Kreon whipped that steel off his hip and waved that mothafucka around at all of those that opposed them. His face was fixed with a scowl and his jaws were clenched, pulsating.

"Whoa! Whoa! Whoa! Back the fuck up!" Kreon roared, spittle flying from off his lips. His hateful eyes studying the cock suckas before him, most of them had their hands up and were mad-dogging him. He didn't give a mad ass fuck though; if they made a move, then he was going to send a couple of them to Satan's house.

"You a dead man, homeboy," Po gritted.

Kreon whipped out his car keys and passed them to Odette, telling her to get the car and pull up in front of the apartment complex. She went off to do as he had commanded, while he stepped up into Po's face. Abruptly, he kicked him in the nuts and doubled him over, eyes tearing. Next, he whacked him upside the head and dropped him in the driveway. Hearing someone trying to run up on him, he whipped around and pointed his banger into their face. It was Tranisha. That shit froze her in place and she looked scared than a bitch, shivering and shit. Smiling sinisterly, Kreon blew her a kiss and slowly backed away until he was in the street, where Odette sat in his car waiting for him. Seeing him approaching, she hurriedly opened the door and he jumped inside. He pulled his leg inside and slammed the door afterwards, giving his boo the word to pull off. As soon as the word was given, she was speeding down the street.

When they got to the end of the block, Kreon looked her over and saw the tears misting in her eyes. Her bottom lip quivered and he grasped her thigh affectionately.

"You all right, Mocha?" he asked, concerned.

She shut her eyelids briefly and nodded her head rapidly. "Yeah, I will be."

"Good." He glanced over his shoulder but didn't see Po and his boys on them. This put him at ease for the time being, but he still didn't allow himself to get too relaxed. He was from the hood, so he knew better than to let his guard down. The shit could get popping again when you thought that it had died down.   And it was just like he thought.

"Babe, they coming!" Odette panicked, seeing a vehicle speeding up behind them in the rearview mirror.

"What?" He frowned.

"That's them behind us. The olive-green Corsica," she whined, tears threatening to spill.

Kreon looked over his shoulder and, as sure as his ass was black, there was an olive-green Corsica speeding up behind them.

"Shit, that is them." He turned back around and checked the chamber of his revolver; it was fully loaded. He smacked that thang shut and tightened his grip on it. "Alright, you see this next light coming up?" He nodded to the stop light ahead. It was yellow and about to turn red. Odette nodded her acknowledgment of the stop light coming up.

"Smooth, they drivin' up fast on the side of us. Once I tell you to, slam on the brakes and lean over into my lap as far as you can. When I get off, mash the pedal and I'ma steer us up outta here, you griff me?" She nodded yes, tears cascading down her face. "Okay." He glanced up in the rearview mirror and saw the pursuing vehicle speeding up alongside of them. "Now!" he barked the order and she slammed on the brakes, ducking down in her man's lap. The Corsica came to a stop beside them. A mad-dogging Kreon pointed his ratchet at the nigga sitting in the front passenger seat.

"This what chu mothafuckaz wanted?" Kreon scowled, applying pressure to the revolver's trigger.

To Be Continued...
God Bless the Trappers 2
Coming Soon

Submission Guideline

Submit the first three chapters of your completed manuscript to ldpsubmissions@gmail.com, subject line: Your book's title. The manuscript must be in a .doc file and sent as an attachment. Document should be in Times New Roman, double spaced and in size 12 font. Also, provide your synopsis and full contact information. If sending multiple submissions, they must each be in a separate email.

Have a story but no way to send it electronically? You can still submit to LDP/Ca$h Presents. Send in the first three chapters, written or typed, of your completed manuscript to:

LDP: Submissions Dept
Po Box 870494
Mesquite, Tx 75187

DO NOT send original manuscript. Must be a duplicate.

Provide your synopsis and a cover letter containing your full contact information.

Thanks for considering LDP and Ca$h Presents.

Coming Soon from Lock Down Publications/Ca$h Presents

BOW DOWN TO MY GANGSTA

By **Ca$h**

TORN BETWEEN TWO

By **Coffee**

BLOOD STAINS OF A SHOTTA **III**

By **Jamaica**

STEADY MOBBIN **III**

By **Marcellus Allen**

BLOOD OF A BOSS **V**

By **Askari**

LOYAL TO THE GAME **IV**

LIFE OF SIN

By **T.J. & Jelissa**

A DOPEBOY'S PRAYER **II**

By **Eddie "Wolf" Lee**

IF LOVING YOU IS WRONG… **III**

LOVE ME EVEN WHEN IT HURTS **II**

By **Jelissa**

TRUE SAVAGE **VI**

By **Chris Green**

BLAST FOR ME **III**

A BRONX TALE

By **Ghost**

ADDICTIED TO THE DRAMA **III**

By **Jamila Mathis**

LIPSTICK KILLAH **III**

CRIME OF PASSION **II**

By **Mimi**

WHAT BAD BITCHES DO **III**

KILL ZONE **II**

By **Aryanna**

THE COST OF LOYALTY **II**

By **Kweli**

SHE FELL IN LOVE WITH A REAL ONE **II**

By **Tamara Butler**

LOVE SHOULDN'T HURT **III**

RENEGADE BOYS **II**

By **Meesha**

CORRUPTED BY A GANGSTA **IV**

By **Destiny Skai**

A GANGSTER'S CODE **III**

By **J-Blunt**

KING OF NEW YORK III

By **T.J. Edwards**

CUM FOR ME **IV**

By **Ca$h & Company**

GORILLAS IN THE BAY

De'Kari

THE STREETS ARE CALLING

Duquie Wilson

KINGPIN KILLAZ II

Hood Rich

STEADY MOBBIN' **III**

Marcellus Allen

SINS OF A HUSTLA **II**

ASAD

HER MAN, MINE'S TOO **II**

Nicole Goosby

GORILLAZ IN THE BAY **II**

DE'KARI

TRIGGADALE II

Elijah R. Freeman

THE STREETS ARE CALLING **II**

Duquie Wilson

Available Now

RESTRAINING ORDER **I & II**

By **CA$H & Coffee**

LOVE KNOWS NO BOUNDARIES **I II & III**

By **Coffee**

RAISED AS A GOON I, II, III & IV

BRED BY THE SLUMS I, II, III

BLAST FOR ME I & II

ROTTEN TO THE CORE I III

By **Ghost**

LAY IT DOWN **I & II**

LAST OF A DYING BREED

BLOOD STAINS OF A SHOTTA I & II

By **Jamaica**

LOYAL TO THE GAME

LOYAL TO THE GAME II

God Bless the Trappers

LOYAL TO THE GAME III

By **TJ & Jelissa**

BLOODY COMMAS I & II

SKI MASK CARTEL I II & III

KING OF NEW YORK I II

By **T.J. Edwards**

IF LOVING HIM IS WRONG…I & II

LOVE ME EVEN WHEN IT HURTS

By **Jelissa**

WHEN THE STREETS CLAP BACK I & II III

By **Jibril Williams**

A DISTINGUISHED THUG STOLE MY HEART I II & III

LOVE SHOULDN'T HURT I II

RENEGADE BOYS

By **Meesha**

A GANGSTER'S CODE I & II

By J-Blunt

PUSH IT TO THE LIMIT

By **Bre' Hayes**

BLOOD OF A BOSS **I, II, III & IV**

By **Askari**

THE STREETS BLEED MURDER **I, II & III**

THE HEART OF A GANGSTA I II& III

By **Jerry Jackson**

CUM FOR ME

CUM FOR ME 2

CUM FOR ME 3

An **LDP Erotica Collaboration**

Tranay Adams

BRIDE OF A HUSTLA **I II & II**

THE FETTI GIRLS **I, II& III**

CORRUPTED BY A GANGSTA I, II & III

By **Destiny Skai**

WHEN A GOOD GIRL GOES BAD

By **Adrienne**

A GANGSTER'S REVENGE **I II III & IV**

THE BOSS MAN'S DAUGHTERS

THE BOSS MAN'S DAUGHTERS II

THE BOSSMAN'S DAUGHTERS III

THE BOSSMAN'S DAUGHTERS IV

THE BOSS MAN'S DAUGHTERS **V**

A SAVAGE LOVE **I & II**

BAE BELONGS TO ME

A HUSTLER'S DECEIT I, II

WHAT BAD BITCHES DO I, II

By **Aryanna**

A KINGPIN'S AMBITON

A KINGPIN'S AMBITION **II**

I MURDER FOR THE DOUGH

By **Ambitious**

TRUE SAVAGE

TRUE SAVAGE II

TRUE SAVAGE **III**

TRUE SAVAGE **IV**

TRUE SAVAGE **V**

By **Chris Green**

A DOPEBOY'S PRAYER

God Bless the Trappers

By **Eddie "Wolf" Lee**

THE KING CARTEL **I, II & III**

By **Frank Gresham**

THESE NIGGAS AIN'T LOYAL **I, II & III**

By **Nikki Tee**

GANGSTA SHYT **I II &III**

By **CATO**

THE ULTIMATE BETRAYAL

By **Phoenix**

BOSS'N UP **I , II & III**

By **Royal Nicole**

I LOVE YOU TO DEATH

By **Destiny J**

I RIDE FOR MY HITTA

I STILL RIDE FOR MY HITTA

By **Misty Holt**

LOVE & CHASIN' PAPER

By **Qay Crockett**

TO DIE IN VAIN

By **ASAD**

BROOKLYN HUSTLAZ

By **Boogsy Morina**

BROOKLYN ON LOCK I & II

By **Sonovia**

GANGSTA CITY

By **Teddy Duke**

A DRUG KING AND HIS DIAMOND I & II III

A DOPEMAN'S RICHES

HER MAN, MINE'S TOO

By Nicole Goosby

TRAPHOUSE KING **I II & III**

KINGPIN KILLAZ

By **Hood Rich**

LIPSTICK KILLAH **I, II**

CRIME OF PASSION

By **Mimi**

STEADY MOBBN' **I, II**

By **Marcellus Allen**

WHO SHOT YA **I, II**

Renta

GORILLAZ IN THE BAY

DE'KARI

TRIGGADALE

Elijah R. Freeman

GOD BLESS THE TRAPPERS I, II, III

THESE SCANDALOUS STREETS I, II, III

FEAR MY GANGSTA I, II

THESE STREETS DON'T LOVE NOBODY I, II

Tranay Adams

THE STREETS ARE CALLING

Duquie Wilson

SINS OF A HUSTLA

ASAD

BOOKS BY LDP'S CEO, CA$H

TRUST IN NO MAN

TRUST IN NO MAN 2

TRUST IN NO MAN 3

BONDED BY BLOOD

SHORTY GOT A THUG

THUGS CRY

THUGS CRY 2

THUGS CRY 3

TRUST NO BITCH

TRUST NO BITCH 2

TRUST NO BITCH 3

TIL MY CASKET DROPS

RESTRAINING ORDER

RESTRAINING ORDER 2

IN LOVE WITH A CONVICT

Coming Soon

BONDED BY BLOOD 2

BOW DOWN TO MY GANGSTA

God Bless the Trappers

Tranay Adams